THRILLVILLE, USA

TAYLOR KOEKKOEK

SIMON & SCHUSTER PAPERBACKS

NEW YORK   LONDON   TORONTO   SYDNEY   NEW DELHI

Simon & Schuster Paperbacks
An Imprint of Simon & Schuster, Inc.
1230 Avenue of the Americas
New York, NY 10020

The following stories were previously published: "Dirtnap" in the *Paris Review*; "Thrillville, USA" in *Glimmer Train*; "The Drowned Woman" in *Witness*; "The Wedding Party" in the *Iowa Review*; "Emergency Maneuvers" in *Ploughshares*; and "The Flight Instructor" in the *Southampton Review*.

First Simon & Schuster trade paperback edition March 2023

For information about special discounts for bulk purchases, please contact Simon & Schuster Special Sales at 1-866-506-1949 or business@simonandschuster.com.

The Simon & Schuster Speakers Bureau can bring authors to your live event. For more information or to book an event, contact the Simon & Schuster Speakers Bureau at 1-866-248-3049 or visit our website at www.simonspeakers.com.

Interior design by Carly Loman

Manufactured in the United States of America

10 9 8 7 6 5 4 3 2 1

Library of Congress Cataloging-in-Publication Data is available on file.

ISBN 978-1-9821-5561-2
ISBN 978-1-9821-5563-6 (ebook)

I wrote these stories to impress my wife, Joselyn.
Thank God for her.

CONTENTS

THRILLVILLE, USA

I N THE FIRST week of the last season at Thrillville, USA, a boy got all fucked-up in the Haunted Mine. The animatronics tore a wasp nest apart somehow, and the kid came out stung to hell. Poor kid was riding alone, too. I'd always thought you could slip from the lap bar if you really wanted to, but I guess not. The minecart lurched out to the loading zone with this kid shrieking his head off, all pink and lumpy, a face pinpricked with bruised dots of blood. Denny and I didn't have any clue what to make of it at first. This deranged, swollen child shrieking like a cat set on fire. Then Glenn with his prosthetic leg came vaulting up on his forearm crutch, shouting for us to kill the ride and release the lap bar already.

It took us a while to figure out what had happened. The kid didn't know those were wasps that attacked in the dark. He believed the Haunted Mine was really haunted, and with such conviction that I felt a bit skittish around the ride afterward. Glenn and I had to walk through the Haunted Mine with flashlights and find the shredded wasp nest buzzing to realize what had happened. I got stung on the hand. The kid was hospitalized, but he was okay. Glenn settled it out of court. He knew the kid's mother. They'd been sleeping together. She used to hang around and he'd made a point of introducing her to

1

everyone. She and Glenn strolled about, sometimes disappearing into his office trailer while the kid roamed the park off-leash. Glenn didn't move too well and he carried some extra weight on him, but he was never without a girlfriend for the moment. We'd met a few of his short-stint lovers by then. He was a good guy, but we guessed it was the leg, the missing one.

"I mean, he looked bad," I told Jen. "Really fucked. Probably he got stung in the eyes."

"How bad though?" she asked. "Like medical-wise?"

"I don't know what you want from me," I told her. I was so hungover, the whole day felt like an anxiety hallucination. "It looked like a pissed-off witch doctor just went to town with a needle on like a little voodoo doll version of the kid."

"Oh my God."

Denny said if voodoo were real he'd carry a little doll version of himself around and jerk it off and lick its ass all day. He knew the kind of jokes I liked and told them, watching me from the corner of his eye. He was my very tallest friend. When he was drunk, he tossed me around like a little dog. It was great. Jen told Denny to grow up. The ambulance hadn't even left yet, she reminded us. That was the boy's mom in hysterics with the paramedics.

Jen glowered at Denny with an expression that seemed to say, you're just the worst, babe. The two of them were having a secret affair that everyone knew about. My least favorite part of the affair was that I had to play clueless about it, although Denny had clued me in from the start. Denny, right after their first night together, told me *all*, too much—the noises she made, the color of her nipples—but Jen, he insisted, wasn't to know that I knew. So they fiddled with each other's genitals when they were at one side of the game counter and me at the other. I couldn't see the action, but I knew what was happening down there. Their mouths were half-open and eyes half-closed. Denny and Jen thought they were doing the most interesting thing in the world together. When they touched, they seemed amazed that something hadn't stopped them from touching. Nobody cared at all, but to them it was magic.

One time, Denny was on a bender and I was having trouble hunting him down, and I asked Jen where he was. It troubled her that I expected she'd know Denny's whereabouts. "I'm not his keeper," she said, indignant, as if I were the one who should be embarrassed, just for knowing the facts, just for being anyone other than the most ignorant person in the room.

Denny was seeing a high schooler then. Girl named Katie. She was pretty and freckled, but she was too young, legally speaking, so they just kissed cheeks, he said, and sent each other dirty texts. "Sow the seed," he told me, "and pluck the tomato a little sour, little green, before anyone else takes it for their own caprese." Then he kissed his pinched fingertips with a big "Muah." He often used nonsense gardening metaphors to talk about Katie. Shucked corn and mushy peaches, et cetera. It was all geared toward the eventual eating of something. He was twenty-five and she was sixteen. One night, when Denny was super fucked, he told me they did hand stuff sometimes, but when he sobered up the next day, he said he was just joking.

Maybe Jen was not quite as pretty as Katie, Denny theorized, but that might have been a virtue of Katie's leg up on her youth-wise. I was a poor audience on this subject because I believed Jen and Katie, between the two of them, had more prettiness than Denny warranted. Jen's hair was so black that, right when I met her, I decided everyone

I'd ever thought of as having black hair really had very dark brown hair. And she was mean, too. I loved that. Jen was technically married to a badass Mexican guy from Salem. He had a left shoulder full of cigarette burns. Dozens of mottled, ring-shaped scars overlaid like a gory octopus arm. He burned himself whenever he drank too much, even though no one had dared him to since middle school. He and Jen had a courthouse marriage in a spur-of-the-moment situation just before he shipped off on his first deployment. They didn't talk anymore, but they were man and wife in the legal sense and in the eyes of the Lord.

What inconvenienced me though, about the affair, was that I'd had to move out of the one-bedroom apartment Denny and I shared. It made getting to work a hassle if I missed my ride with Glenn, since Denny and I'd gone in together on an old, two-hundred-dollar Ford Pinto. We loved it. We drove it around like a go-cart. The rear bumper was torn up like a busted lip and the front bumper just dropped off one night on its own. Technically Denny and I shared custody, but mostly he kept it. I was reasonable about parting with the Pinto and apartment both. The apartment lease was in Denny's name, and it was his mom that helped with rent. It was her old raggedy sofa I slept on, too. Fair was fair. Denny'd told me his stepbrother was moving back to Turner, and needed help getting on his feet, but then his stepbrother never showed up and Jen was always over, her clothes on the bedroom floor, beauty stuff all over the sink rim, strands of her long black hair in the drain. I put it together. Glenn let me crash on his couch. It wasn't like I was out on the street. He had a massive old tube TV and a bachelorly place in the mobile home park at the next exit down I-5.

The foot was the first thing I noticed about Glenn when we met a few years before. It didn't move right. I was only twenty-one then. I asked if his foot was fake during my interview. He said that's poor interview etiquette. Then he bent forward conspiratorially and hiked up the cuff of his jeans so I could get an eye on the metal prosthesis. He told me that in the nineties he was hand propping his ex-brother-in-law's Cessna, but when he yanked the motor running, the brake block beneath the tire must have jimmied loose because the airplane budged forward just a hair and the prop caught him right above the ankle. He said it flipped him a rotation and a half onto his head and it shot his foot across the hangar bay with such force it dented the hangar wall. "The foot," he said solemnly, "exploded." He took painkillers for his phantom limb pains. Some days it felt like his foot was still there, he said, ghost toes wiggling on command, but it also felt like the foot was pinched in a vise. The pain flared up when he was stressed-out or lonesome or feeling ashamed, which accounted for all his time on earth. Denny and I figured he probably just had a pill problem like everyone else we knew, but we left him his story because, first off, we partied too and, secondly, because we liked Glenn, and also because Denny snuck us pills now and again from Glenn's stash. Glenn kept his pills in his office desk. He didn't like to keep his meds on him because he ended up relying on them too much, he said. I told him, sure, the desk was a fine stowing place.

GLENN HAD OWNED Thrillville, USA for four years then, and each year of business was a miracle. The wasp incident was terrible timing. It came on the heels of another bad one. The previous season a heavy drunk managed to launch himself from the Magic Carpet Slide, then plummeted a floor and a half down to a concrete walkway. We didn't think that was even possible, but then the guy came soaring overhead with his shirt off. Cracked his pelvis clean through. Messed his pants on impact, instantaneously. He messed his pants so fast, we thought the mess in his pants might have been a preexisting condition. I'm making light of this now, but it was really a horrific thing to witness.

Insurance and maintenance would have been enough trouble, but park attendance was at an all-time low. We broke low attendance records every month. We shut down midday all the time. Stood attendant to the idling rides, humming and vibrating for no riders. Money vanished into the park as into a pocket with a hole in it. Glenn, though, even desperate as he must have been, seemed to grow more affectionate toward the place with the loss of every dollar.

Before Thrillville, Glenn ran a carpet cleaning business that did okay for a while before it went out. He opened a bait and tackle shop once by the reservoir, but that was practically DOA. He said he wished he knew how to work for someone else, but he was always the first guy fired. Glenn was left by two patient women in his life, though they remained on friendly terms. Some days they brought him meals wrapped in foil. They worried about him. It had always seemed obvious to me that Thrillville wasn't built to last, and that Glenn had practiced his whole life to see it off. He was its perfect hospice worker. Or he was like the servant who buries himself alive with the pharaoh.

Thrillville, USA had been owned by a series of unlucky men over the years. Each built additions without any thought of continuity, a total thematic fiasco. The feeling it had was like some madman's roadside collection of carnival antiques. At the southern side, nearest the interstate, there was a sort of fairy-tales thing going on—the Magic Carpet Ride, Enchanted Forest, and Haunted Mine. Up above that, the park phased into an indiscriminate mix of Greek and Roman mythology, starting with the Flight of Icarus, which flew not at all, but instead spun passengers around and around and was generally considered a terrible time. Neptune's Wrath, our one water attraction, which you could see from the parking lot, spiraling five or six times above the fence. No one rode it. Wasn't worth the toweling off and change of clothes. At the other end there was the Screamin' Eagle, which might have been patriotic, except it sat opposite the Cuckoo Ka-Choo, so maybe it was just avian. Glenn hadn't added any attractions in his tenure, except for a new photobooth and a penny press machine, which mashed pennies into ovals, thin as a toenail. The machine imprinted the pennies with THRILLVILLE, USA SINCE 1977. Denny loved to watch the penny press work. He thought it was like a magic trick. He said, "You gotta spend money to make money." But he said that all the time. Buying a beer at the Golden Nugget, buying a pair of shiny orange bowling shoes at the Salvation Army: *gotta spend money to make money.*

Glenn decided to host a fireworks night every second Friday of the month for that summer season. We shut all the rides off, except for the Ferris wheel and the Rock-O-Plane cages so that visitors could be drawn in from the highway by the flashing passenger carriages. That was fanciful thinking, I said. The surrounding county was ready, had long been ready, made its demands of the city council already, for Thrillville to shut down. It was, by popular opinion, an eyesore, a noise pollutant, and a death trap. They would be glad to see it gone, and to see us gone with it.

* * *

THRILLVILLE, USA

THAT FIRST FIREWORKS Friday, I was turning down the Ripper, the oldest steel coaster in Oregon over such and such height—or so claimed Glenn anyway. By now it was fairly run-down, and you heard plenty of rumors about it. According to one rumor, the coaster cars beat so violently around the curves that a woman once lost her pregnancy at the first turn. In another version of the story, the unborn baby was a young boy who, while riding with his mother in the rearmost car, was flung from his seat at the turn and scattered dead into the parking lot. If any of that was remotely true, I think I'd have heard about it from Glenn. I removed the pocket trash from the footwells, then wetted a rag with disinfectant and rubbed down the seats, the asswells—shaped in such an impression as I have never met a living ass to match—then the shoulder bars, the buckles, so on, before I called it satisfactory and hit the lights out. I spent the next quarter hour wandering around beneath the coaster with a flashlight, looking for dropped wallets and cell phones. If any jewelry ever turned up, it was the faux, plastic stuff. I didn't find anything this night except a flip-flop, which I left floating upturned in the small, leechy pond.

Denny was sneaking himself between the park, where Jen saved him a spot on the yellow lawn, and the untenanted gravel lot that lay adjacent to Thrillville. A dozen high schoolers assembled a bonfire there and ringed their parents' cars around it and laid out on the hoods to watch the fireworks. Katie was there, hoping Denny would sneak off with her for the finale. I told Glenn those high schoolers were seeing the show for free. Glenn didn't mind. He thought it was a step in the right direction.

We'd set floodlights up around the concessions pavilion, and with the lights placed down low and angled upward, they had strange shadows dancing around in the dusty evening. Glenn was messing around in the launch zone, which he'd stanchioned off and fixed with hand-written warning signs. Andy, a rail-thin seventeen-year-old who'd started at Thrillville partway through the previous season, was selling beer on the down-low out of a cooler for three dollars apiece. He was drunk early. When he was drunk, he winked a lot and drew a finger gun and clicked his tongue.

"That little alien dude does a shit human impression," Denny said.

I went back through the park to stake my spot for the show and came across a low rustling in the dirt along the back side of the Scrambler. I pointed my flashlight at the noise and clicked it on, and in the sudden brightness two teenagers materialized, groping each other passionately. The guy rose up on an elbow and shielded his eyes. He called out, "Whoa whoa, man, get outta here!" I stood there blinking at them, shining my light in their eyes. The squinting girl giggled in a low tank top and held herself. I saw the bluish color of veins in her pale chest. That killed me for some reason. The guy gathered himself upright, huffing indignantly, and he told the girl to come on, and they darted off into the dark like a pair of deer.

I hung around fidgeting for a while, electrified with longing and shame in equal parts. Then it occurred to me: It was those two that were behaving badly, wasn't it? That audacious horndog had scolded me as if I'd barged into his dorm room, but they were the ones fooling around in my place of business. I decided I'd find them, tell them the score, or maybe just keep an eye on them. I didn't know what I meant to do, but I was already on the move. I had something to live for all of a sudden. Far off in the distance there were voices speaking in that tone they speak in when a show is about to begin.

I'd nearly given up the search when I heard one high, clear note of laughter ring out from the Magic Carpet Slide then vanish beneath the low hum of Thrillville, USA. I switched off my light. The slide was eight-lanes-wide yellow fiberglass and descended to the earth in a series of gentle waves. The underside was all cobwebbed rafters and beams like the space beneath a set of bleachers. Now and then Denny got lit and nodded off beneath the slide. He told me he'd once come upon shadowy figures humping each other under there. The trouble now was the lighting. I edged up around a corner of the slide and crouched by a buggy shrub and trained my eyes blindly at where the action sounded to be. I felt light-headed. It sounded like chewing. It sounded like they were eating each other alive.

Then the first mortar reported overhead, and the sky exploded with golden light and then green light, red light, blue. One flash at a time, I saw the teenagers pulling at each other's vulnerables. The reports grew in frequency and choked the sky with light and the eggy smell of combustion. I felt the mortar concussions in my chest, like ka-kunk ka-kunk. And my heart doing something similar, ka-kunk, ka-kunk. The boy spread himself over the girl as if he meant to cover her entirely, the way a soldier jumps on a live grenade lobbed into the bunker, like in the movies. And then, in the fiery light, the girl adjusted herself, turned beneath her lover, and I saw her illuminated. She lay her head in the golden nest of her hair, and her face was the golden baby bird of a face, and it was perfect absolutely. She had one of her pale breasts out and her boyfriend held on to it for dear life. Of course, I lit up too. Like the lighted statue of a pervert. I saw her and then she saw me, unmade, each of us, into the dark every other second, made back again in the light. She patted her boyfriend in a panic. "He's back," she said.

"Where?" he said, spinning his head.

"There," she said. "That's him."

They rose again and ducked out from beneath the slide. "Why won't you fuck off?" the guy said as they passed, holding hands. The girl didn't even glance up at me as they went, and before I could apologize, they were gone. I sat slumped beneath the booming sky and felt flat-out rotten about myself. Then the show ended, and everyone went home.

"SEE," GLENN TOLD me at the house, "I knew a firework show wouldn't be so hard to set up. It's a scam—all the permits, the paperwork." Without any mind paid to legal or regulatory processes, Glenn had taken a Tuesday and trekked out north to the Chehalis reservation in Washington, where the fireworks that were illegal in Oregon in any season were sold year-round. "Next time I'm thinking we might put the show to music."

I shrugged. "I mean, knock yourself out."

"Yeah. Okay," he said. "I will." Then he was quiet for a while. "You're probably right."

"About what?"

"None of this makes a difference, does it?"

I told him I didn't mean anything by it. And he told me it didn't make a difference anyway.

So we kicked our shoes off and slumped into the couch and watched his behemoth TV. He'd seemed bummed to me for the last few days. It was more than just the financial straits. At close each night he walked around Thrillville with a heartbroken smile as though he'd just finished reading a long, sad book about love. "Think I'll give her the once-over," he'd say. "I'll meet you at the car." Seeing Glenn low messed with my buzz.

So I asked him what gives. Maybe it was the wasp incident, something about the kid's mother, I thought, but no. Glenn said there was a girl he'd loved when he was a kid. He'd always thought that he'd see her again somewhere down the line, and who knows, maybe things would finally click. So then last week he thought to himself, "I own my own business, right? Got the respect and admiration from my employees. Still one good foot. Shoot, next year I'll probably have less than I do this year. That's been the way of things." In a manic spell of bravery, he'd looked her up on the internet, guessing she was probably married, but it turned out she had died of a heart infection in the mid-nineties.

"Holy cow," I said.

"I know it's terrible, but the whole time I keep thinking, what did I lose, then? Because it feels like I lost something, me personally, but I can't quite put my finger on it. Nothing seems to have really changed for me, on the day-to-day, but I have this feeling now like my life is over. Or like it's been over for a long time and I'm just now realizing it. I always had this feeling like the real thing was about to begin."

"That's a tough one," I said. "That'd fuck anyone up."

"Yeah, I think it must have messed me up."

Then Glenn winced and I asked what was wrong. "Foot," he said. I asked what was wrong with his foot. "No, the left one," he said, tapping his left knee.

"Oh. Right."

"It wouldn't be so bad," he said, "the phantom sensations. But the pain. It wouldn't be so bad if it didn't feel like a dog was chewing on it all the time. Otherwise I might find some comfort in it, even. Like, close my eyes and think, yeah, still there."

Then I learned that Glenn had recently swapped meds. His doctor switched him from short-release Vicodin tablets to long-release fentanyl patches. He showed me one of them, and then thumbed it delicately onto his arm. The patches had a sort of opiate jelly inside. He told me not to tell Denny about them. "You gotta be careful Denny's not a bad influence on you," he said. "Why?" he asked. "Well, all I know is, I see you on the one hand, right, my best employee. The best employee I ever had in all my enterprises. Honest to God, Coop. And you know who's my worst employee?"

"Who?"

"Come on," he said.

I asked what'd Denny ever done that was so bad. Glenn scoffed and said just last week Denny barfed on some kid's sandals, which was true. No way around it. "Okay," I said. "But what've I ever done right, then?" Because I'd barfed on a lady's handbag one time at the Lancaster Mall and I felt awful about it. I thought it had the ring of the one small last thing that would tip the scales and send me to hell.

"You're a quick thinker, Cooper," he said. "You're not afraid to take action." I asked Glenn for an example. He said, didn't I remember when I shut down the Haunted Mine to help that kid out? Saved the day. "That was quick thinking."

"I only stopped the ride when you told me to, though."

"Yeah, exactly. You stopped the ride exactly when I said so. You took action. Denny doesn't take action. Denny's idea of action is stealing my meds. I know a little something about what's going on under my own nose. What am I gonna do, get the kid arrested? Those aren't just party favors, Coop. I need them. Look, I love that kid, but he doesn't have any folds in his brain." Glenn said he knew he should just leave his meds locked in his car, but the walk was a pain on his prosthesis. He was running out of hiding places in the office. "I don't know how Denny does it. Doesn't matter where I hide them. He's got a sixth sense for it." I said he could try the little freezer on his office fridge.

He wasn't going to give me one of his patches, but I dogged him into it eventually, and then we split a pack of tallboys and we both had patches on our arms. Later, Glenn went to bed, and I slept where I usually did on the sofa. I felt like I was floating in warm, black water. And like the dark was throbbing around me with my heartbeat. And then it felt like the couch was breathing beneath me. It was like I laid my head on a giant, benevolent chest that was breathing. Then I slept like a dead man.

THAT FIRST FIREWORKS Friday resulted in a modest bump in business. No one but Glenn had actually guessed it'd have any effect, but we didn't close down midday all through the rest of June except for twice. Glenn even wanted to talk about the long-term future of Thrillville, which I thought was sort of dubious, but I indulged him. He drafted wonky expansion designs on a pad of graph paper. I didn't know about those. Glenn lacked spatial reasoning or something.

We did our internet research and went to FedEx and doctored some papers to look like a permit for a fireworks show. Nothing too convincing, but enough to flash the sheriff if he showed up with questions. The sheriff did come around, too, but he came with his wife and told Glenn he wasn't there in any official capacity. "If you blow yourself up, I'll treat it like part of the show."

I didn't have cash on me and I wanted another beer, but Andy wouldn't float me any more freebies from the cooler. I wasn't about to ask Glenn for cash, though, because I promised him I'd be no-funny-business until the show concluded, plus he was liable to shut down Andy's operation if he caught a whiff of it. Then Denny walked up in some sort of daze and patted a kid's head, who then looked at his mother like, Did you see that? But she hadn't seen. Denny tried to sit down on Andy's cooler, and Andy shooed him away. So Denny backed up alongside me saying, "All right, little guy. Keep it holstered." He leaned up against the concession stand wall and crossed an ankle over the other, then tweaked my nipples through my T-shirt. I told him he looked fucked-up. He asked if he'd look cooler smoking.

"Katie out at the bonfire?" I asked.

"She just left."

"Before the show?"

"I guess so, man."

I asked what for. Denny said Katie had seen him in the Pinto with Jen.

"That's bad," I said. "What'd she see?"

"She got an eyeful, anyway." Denny said he'd been going down on Jen in the back seat, his pants already off—this was a reciprocal situation being made good on—his bare ass backed up to the window, which turned out to be the window that Katie peered into through her cupped hand. Denny seemed to think something over. Then he told me, "Like, I always said she was more mature than us, you know, and maybe she is, but now I'm thinking I also said that because I knew she was too much a kid still."

"Yeah. That sounds right."

"She just kept asking like what'd she do wrong."

"Poor girl."

"Yeah," he said. "Poor Katie."

Denny stared into the floodlight. He said, "I wonder what's like the meanest thing I ever said about you. You know?" I told him to knock it off. "No, no," he said. "Not like to your face, I mean. Like, just about you. To someone else. Like, what's the meanest thing I've said about you when you weren't there to get all butthurt?"

"Yeah, I get it already."

"Yeah, yeah," he said, then seemed to think. A couple teenaged girls huddled up to Andy nervously and he sold them two beers for the price of one. Then Andy turned to me and asked what I was looking at. He already gave me two freebies and two loaners. Then Denny went on, "I guess sometimes when we meet new people, I just want them to like me better than they like you. Does that make sense? Especially if it's a girl. Is that just like human?"

And I said, "Yeah, I get you, Denny. You don't have to explain more."

"Yeah," he said. "You get me."

"Christ. Where's Jen at anyway?"

"I think she's messed up about the Katie thing."

I asked if he was going to go track her down and he said yeah, maybe he would. Then he said, "There was this one time, like *early* early on, Jen asked me about you, like your qualities, and I said, yeah, Coop's an okay-enough guy, but if I never see him again, I won't miss him. I said we're only friends because we like getting messed up the same amount. That would've stung if you'd overheard."

"Yeah," I said. "I guess it would."

"Makes you wonder what the meanest thing someone who isn't your best friend said about you. You know? Had to be brutal."

Denny kept staring into that floodlight, swaying a little in his boots. Gnats appeared and disappeared in and out of the slanted column of yellow light.

"How you feeling, Denny?" I asked. "You look especially fucked."

"Me, in a word, Coop: prettygood."

He said I'd been right about the mini fridge. Glenn's stash of fentanyl was in the freezer compartment. He said the patches were like tiny slushy packs. He said the goo inside tasted awful.

"I think I tore the package a little. Hope Glenn doesn't notice."

I told Denny he better steer clear of Glenn until he wasn't so messed up. "We're testing his patience, I think." Denny said he'd go chill out somewhere. I told him to sleep it off in the Pinto. Denny started to go and I asked him, before he went, did he have any beer money.

"You dog, you," he said, and rummaged in his pocket. He offered me three pressed pennies. He jostled them around in his palm.

"What for?"

"For a brew, blockhead."

I told him a beer was three dollars.

"It costs a dollar to make a pressed penny, plus the penny."

"Why'd you spend three dollars on these?"

"Three dollars and three cents," he said.

"Sure, but why?"

"Gotta spend money to make money, man."

Denny tipped the pennies into my hand and kissed my forehead with a loud smack. Then he pointed upward, and I think he tried to tell me something about the sky, but he couldn't make himself clear. He kept calling it the ceiling. "Listen," he said, "I know exactly how God felt when he made the ceiling because that's how I feel when I look at the ceiling, and when I look at the ceiling I feel so lonely!" Denny waited to see if I understood, but I didn't, so he shrugged and wandered off.

GLENN SAID I only had two responsibilities during the firework show. First, I was supposed to start the music on his mark. He asked me to guess the music, and I said I'd rather it be a surprise, and he loved that. What was the second responsibility, I asked Glenn. "Find a perfect seat and take it all in," he told me, grinning. Also, he said to take some mental notes if any improvements occurred to me. It was high time I started pulling some of the strings around here. I went back to Andy and told him, when Glenn signaled for the music over the walkie, I needed him to press play on the sound system for me. I showed him the button and clicked my walkie off. Andy winked, finger-gunned me. "Got you covered."

I eyed Andy for a moment and then told him if he didn't give me another beer I'd tell Glenn about his operation. He looked up at me with heartbreak in his eyes. But I trusted you, is what his expression seemed to say, though he only stood there, searching my face over for something. I never had brothers—just one sister—and I wondered now, was this how a little brother looks at an older brother after a wedgie or a nut kick or whatnot? Andy hung his head and turned and he lifted a beer from the cooler, a tallboy too, God bless him, and he held that out to me. I looked at the beer.

"Ah, shit, I was kidding," I told him. "I was only kidding, Andy."

Andy smiled and nodded. "Okay," he said. "Yeah, okay, Coop."

Then I left the lawn. I went off through the central corridor of Thrillville, looking for wallets, looking for phones, and in particular I was looking for teens fooling around again. I couldn't help myself. A man hard at work. I absolutely did not think a pair of teens would invite me to join in their lovemaking. There was no reason for it. They had everything they required. They'd have to be crazy. They'd have to be stupid drunk.

Then Jen passed by and asked if I'd seen Denny around.

"He's all whacked out."

"Where?"

I shrugged.

Then I saw that she'd been crying. She tried not to look at me squarely, but I saw she was raw and puffy around the eyes. "Make him call me if you find him, okay?" I said sure and asked if she had any petty cash, but she kept walking. "Hey, Jen," I called. She stopped and turned back. Jen, at that distance, in the darkened aisle, was all shadow, her wet eyes buried darkly in the shape of her face. I wanted to tell her I heard about the Katie incident. I wasn't sure exactly what to say about it. Maybe not to beat herself up too much if she could help it. Or that it was mostly Denny's fault anyway. Or that I thought she was a good person all in all, even though I had a shit barometer for that sort of thing. None of it seemed particularly useful or true. Then a mortar shell whistled up white into the purple night and exploded downfield. Jen lit up blue in all her heartbroken loveliness. "I'll keep an eye out for him," I told her.

Jen nodded, and then she turned and left.

But dammit, Andy, where was the music? Here were the fireworks. Here was the sky very obviously exploding with fireworks, but no music. I knew I was going to catch hell from Glenn. I gave Glenn up in my heart, just like that, and hurried on, thinking of nothing but teenaged lovers. I made my way to the Magic Carpet Slide and stood, shivering, listening for sounds in the dark.

There was not a pair of lovers underneath, but there was someone sitting upright against a support beam. I was too horned up to be surprised or unsurprised. The sky flashed and flashed, and one glimpse at a time I studied the seated figure. Then the music began. "Take Me Home Tonight," that Eddie Money song. The guitar lick throbbed through the mostly empty park. Glenn's favorite song of all time. I could have guessed it. He'd played it at both his weddings, he said, after the vows and kiss and everything. If there were ever a third marriage, he'd play it there, too. "I feel hunger," it went, "It's a hunger that tries to keep a man awake at night."

"Hey," I called out. "Denny, that you?" But there was no stirring.

I ventured in, ducking beneath head-height beams, high-stepping over low beams, negotiating the dusty space like an attic crowded with boxes. Yeah, that was Denny, with his eyes closed and his ankles crossed. I was a little peeved, but not in any way that was defensible. It was like finding a catfish in the crawdad pot and all the crawdads spooked off. Denny and I had once lived on crawdads alone for an entire week just to see if we could. It was great. We caught them in a wire trap and spent hours by the creek telling each other the same jokes, with minor variations, for hours and hours. The thing about it, when you sit like that all day long, smelling the water, feeling the cool air off the water, speaking just to hear the sound of voices—birds are calling in the timbered hills, but you can't see a single one—it's almost like you could forget your own name and that would be A-OK.

"What's wrong with the Pinto?" I asked. "You know the sheriff's here." The trouble would be how to move Denny in such a state without Glenn or the sheriff witnessing anything. I seriously considered leaving him as he was, but I couldn't quite bear that. Imagine Denny coming to alone in the dirt, in an empty Thrillville, behind locked gates. One thing I knew about Denny that most people didn't, was that he cried easily, sometimes for no apparent reason. "All right," I said. "Let's give this a go, then. Up, up." I spoke singsongy as the chorus came on. "Let's take you home tonight." When I kicked his foot, it flopped around like a slab of rubber. Right then—though I'd call his name a few more times, kick him again, shake his shoulders, slap him, and feel for a pulse—I knew Denny was dead.

I SAT THERE for a long time looking at Denny, or at the dimness where he lay, faintly illuminated in the firework flashes, then gone in the dark, back and forth. I watched and hoped in the light he would not reappear. Or I hoped that he would reappear, but he would be risen on his elbow, asking what we were doing in the dirt like a couple of blockheads. We'd see it later that he'd torn a fentanyl patch in half and stuffed it up his nose. Eventually the fireworks ended. The music cut out. The visitors left. They took their distant, happy voices with them. I sat waiting for something else to happen and nothing did. With the passage of every minute, Denny seemed more and more irretrievable to me. I cleared my throat and dried my face on my sleeve and radioed Glenn. "Hey, Glenn," I said, sounding shakier than I'd hoped to. "There's a problem."

"Cooper? Where the heck are you? I swear to God, Coop."

"Shit, Glenn. It's real bad."

"You're messed up, aren't you? You promised me no funny business. You promised, Coop."

There were multiple walkies out there. Andy had one. Jen too. There were half a dozen out there, and I didn't want to broadcast over all of them. Glenn would understand that. "Don't go anywhere," I told him. "I'm coming to you."

I found Glenn and Andy beside a pair of dollies stacked up with crates of mortar launch tubes and a spool of green fuse. Glenn was shouting at Andy, who was wrenched over yacking in the lawn. "You're all a bunch of lowlives!" Glenn shouted. "Everyone messed up all the time. Everyone sucking everyone off all the time. I should fire every one of you and start from scratch." Glenn wetted a paper towel with a water bottle and handed it to Andy. "I'm calling your mom," he said. "I'm sure as heck not driving you home. Maybe Jen will, if you're lucky. Well, I'm sure as heck not. I'm the very last resort. Okay, Andy?" Then he saw me coming. "My God, Coop. What am I supposed to do? I've tried everything with you. Opened my home to you. Help me understand, Coop, because I don't get it. I give you some responsibility, and you hang me out to dry."

I told Glenn he had to come with me.

"You crap all over me, Coop. I don't get it. I don't understand why you do it."

"Okay, Glenn," I said. "I'm an asshole and a lost cause, but you have to come with me now. Fire me after if you want."

"Dammit, Coop. What's so important, then?"

So I showed him.

I WATCHED GLENN blow into Denny's mouth and pump his chest for a good ten minutes until we heard a rib crack, then Glenn gave up and buried his face in his filthy hands. It hadn't occurred to me to try to resuscitate Denny. I don't like to think about that.

"Denny, you big idiot, Denny," Glenn said. "Goddammit." Then we sat for a while longer, beneath the slide's fiberglass underbelly, not saying anything. I lost track of time. Or time came and went. Time wanted nothing to do with me.

Then Glenn said, "Cooper, tell me they weren't mine. Tell me he got it somewhere else."

I couldn't make out Glenn's face, only where it ought to be. I looked at that darkness where his eyes might have been closed or open and I didn't say anything.

"Ah man," he said. He began rocking. "Dammit. I killed him, didn't I?"

I told him it wasn't anyone's fault, but I wasn't convinced by my own voice either. We sat in silence again until I felt a sleepiness shivering over me. I thought we might spend the night with Denny in the dirt. It struck me then, in full force, if I slept there, how exactly I would feel in my first forgetful moment after waking, and then the moment after, when I'd remember everything and I'd turn my head and he would be there and I'd see Denny's face in the daylight. I said I guess we should call the sheriff back.

"What for?" There was panic in Glenn's voice. He rose to a frog squat.

"What do you mean what for?"

"You know how this will go. I lose it all. Thrillville? Thrillville's gone. You see that, right?"

"You don't know that."

"An employee overdoses on my meds on company property?"

"Glenn. Shit," I said. "He's dead. What else can we do?"

"You should head home. I'll meet you there."

"What do you think you'll do when I go?"

"I don't know, Coop."

"You're thinking you'll move him?"

"I don't know."

"Where would you even move him to?"

"Coop, I don't know," he said. "Maybe to the Pinto."

But the Pinto was on company property too, so same difference. Glenn said he'd move that, too, onto the neighboring lot. I expressed my doubts that he could move Denny more than a few feet on his own, not on his prosthesis. Denny must have been forty pounds heavier than Glenn. Plus, the Pinto was a manual, and without a real left foot, Glenn wasn't any good with a clutch. I rummaged through Denny's pockets.

"Coop, what are you doing?"

"Getting the car keys," I said.

"You shouldn't be here. I want you to head home."

I paused with the keys in hand. Then I said I was going to get the car.

GLENN WAITED WITH Denny as I moved the Pinto as close to the slide as possible, beside the Ripper, which left us another thirty yards or so to close on foot. I saw the parking lot was empty. The bonfire in the next lot was empty too. All the teenagers had gone home and left their fire to burn itself out. I parked and stepped out and made my way back under the slide and announced that it was me.

Glenn asked where Jen was.

"Don't know," I said. "Her car's not here. She must be at home."

"Think she'll come back looking?"

"She might."

"Well, there's no sense in taking our time."

We were too scared to use flashlights. We worked in the dark. I scooped Denny up beneath the arms and Glenn took him by the ankles. He was heavy and limp, so we went slow. Denny's ass dragged on the ground and knocked against beams, which sent metallic shudders through the slide. I asked Glenn if he needed a rest, but he said we should just get it over with.

We could move faster once we got out to the paved walkway. Could see better, too. We waddled on with Denny slung between us like a dead man in a hammock. His head dangled back and his mouth was hung open. Glenn retched and halted without warning. Denny's arms yanked from my grasp and he dropped. The back of his head cracked against the pavement like a coconut covered in skin. It was too much for us. I started crying. Glenn too. We gathered Denny up, apologizing to each other, and him, and went weeping to the car.

We opened the Pinto's two back doors and Glenn lifted Denny in as I pulled from the other side. We laid him down on his back and tucked his legs in, then we climbed in front, and I started the car. A phone rang but it was not mine and it was not Glenn's, and we didn't say anything else about it.

We parked at the edge of the gravel flat and waited there, watching. Glenn opened his window and we listened for voices, but there weren't any. He took the clipped fentanyl patch from Denny's nose and found another patch in his pocket. We had to go, Glenn said. It wasn't safe for us to linger there. He paced over the gravel, and I agreed that it was not safe to linger. Then I sat for a while longer, sensing very dimly the momentum with which my feet would hit the ground, and how quickly they would carry me away from this. I sensed how much of this I'd have to leave behind if I was going to leave at all. I looked around. In the gravel there were tossed beer cans. Beer cans stomped down into jagged aluminum disks. The fire crackled in little red bursts. Embers trailed upward spirals in the opening of trees. Denny lay just behind me in perfect silence until his cell phone rang in his pocket again. It rang and rang and then stopped ringing.

WE WENT TO lock up Glenn's office trailer and found the door to the mini fridge ajar and the package of fentanyl torn to shreds, left split on the floor and the patches scattered around. "That damn maniac," Glenn said. "Anyone could have come by." Glenn gathered the patches in a pile on the desk and swept them into an empty Styrofoam cup and snapped a lid on it. Then he rubbed his face on his shirtsleeve and stood there sniffling. We turned the lights out, and I waited as Glenn fumbled with his key and the lock. He kept missing. Then I saw Jen. She came up from the dark, huddled inside an oversized sweatshirt.

"Cooper, he didn't come home."

"Denny didn't?"

"Who else?" Then she looked at Glenn. "Did you see Denny go anywhere?"

"No," Glenn said. He had a coffee cup of opiates in his one hand. His other was shaking with the key ring. "Sorry, Jen."

"Well, the Pinto isn't in the parking lot, and here you are, so Denny went somewhere with it. He won't answer his phone."

"I don't know, Jen," I said.

"Dammit," Jen said. "I'm here picturing he got trashed and drove into a ditch again, you know? I'm picturing him all smashed up somewhere." She looked at us, one then the other. "Why am I the only one freaking out?"

Then Jen turned and left, and we watched her go. From the wooden set of steps that rose to Glenn's office door, we watched Jen walk down the park's central aisle and through the front gate into the nighttime lot. She stepped out a few paces and hesitated, then she stopped. It was as if someone had just called her name from the dark. She stared off at the bonfire flat. Jen turned back to look at us again, or I thought she did. Then she went to see.

WHEN THE AUTHORITIES were finally finished with it, they returned the Pinto to me, and I got another six years out of it before it finally crapped out at the side of a country road outside a high desert town. By then Thrillville was gone and where it had been they'd made another mobile home park. The way I heard it, Glenn's heart just wasn't in it after Denny died. I'd already left Turner by then, and Jen came with me. I phoned her that I was going, and she asked me where to. When I told her I didn't know, she said she wanted to go there. We ran around the Pacific Northwest together for a few years. For eight months we lived by the ocean with a hippie who loved acid, and that was all right. Glenn tried to call me for the first couple years, but eventually he gave up.

Jen's husband, who she'd nearly forgotten by then, wrote her to say that he was AWOL. Jen's mother forwarded just that one letter to her. The seal was broken. Jen's husband wrote that he'd met a young woman in South Carolina and that they were in love and that they would live together with her grandmother in Guadalajara. Jen told me the letter went on but wasn't interesting. He was sweet enough, she said, in his dumb way, but she wouldn't say how. One night Jen was drunk out of her mind, whimpering at dream people in the room, and I took my chance to snoop through the back shelf of the closet, where she kept her secrets. I found the envelope, his writing on it, the letter, and for once I stopped short. This wasn't mine to look at, was it? I didn't have any right, did I? And then I put it all back the way I found it.

Another time, somewhere southeast of Tacoma, Jen and I found ourselves at the edge of an old wood, which lifted out abruptly into a long and bright stretch of farmland. Round bales of hay lay unattended across the high green fields. Behind us a barkless pine lay sidelong, segmented and silvered by age. Jen was going like a gymnast on it, barefoot, her arms outstretched, stepping heel toe. She'd removed her shoes first, almost ceremoniously, I thought. I jogged back to the Pinto and retrieved one of Denny's pressed pennies from the coin tray. All this time, I'd kept them there. I held the penny out to Jen, as a gift or talisman, I didn't quite know. I hoped she would understand. She asked me why in the world I had kept it, then tilted it from her hand into a clover tuft, where I was too embarrassed to go looking for it. Jen was even pregnant for a while, but she didn't have the baby and she told me it wasn't mine anyway, and then one morning she was gone before I woke up. Where she went, I don't know. I've lost track of anyone who would. A week later, I stepped into a bar and emerged three months later at my first rehab clinic.

It wasn't that I'd meant to keep the pennies so long, or that I was even aware of them most of the time. I just never thought to get rid of them. When the Pinto finally died, I took my two bags from the trunk and then I returned to the driver's seat and sat there with the door open and the hood popped, one foot in the car and the other on the road. I looked at the two elongated pennies I had left, mixed up with regular pennies and dimes and gum wrappers and a cigarette that was snapped in half. Then I hiked the fifteen miles to town, where the mechanic guessed it would cost more to tow the car than it was worth. He said, didn't I know, Ford recalled most of the 1970s Pintos decades ago, after the lawsuits and explosions. A shoddy tank design made it so any rear-end collisions could turn the whole thing into a fireball. No, I said. I wasn't aware. So I left it where it lay and what happened to it after that I don't know. Someone hauled it away. Maybe someone saw something in it that I hadn't, because I looked at that old beater and thought there was not one good thing worth keeping.

THE ARTIST'S HOUSE

ZACK HAD AN email in the morning from his agent. I saw on his face the news was bad. What his face said to me was that he had dreaded this news with such singular, sustained focus that he had conjured it forth from his imagination. His manuscript of short stories was rejected by a first round of editors. Waiting in worry of disappointment had already ravaged the mood in our apartment. His agent, I don't know why, spared Zack the rejections individually to present him three at once. I didn't think highly of that. Maybe she was hoping to come back with good news, but it ended up producing quite the wallop. Meanwhile, I was just finishing a final round of novel edits for my publisher. It was an unfortunate confluence of events. I couldn't celebrate as gleefully as I might have, and Zack couldn't wallow with the same abandon. So he's pretending to be happy, I'm pretending to be sad, and we decided to take a little trip, which he called a celebration, and I called a consolation. We planned to meet in good humor somewhere in between. Such are the perils of artists taking up with artists, and such is life: the good things are happening as the bad things are happening, and you have to sign for all of it to receive any of it.

The trip was my idea. In Zack's household, growing up, I knew the family tradition was to go on a little trip whenever tragedy visited his family. When their first dog died, Zack's parents took him and his sister to Seattle for a weekend and spun around in the Space Needle with their waffles and their heartbreak. After his grandfather had his heart attack and drove off the interstate, they went to the coast. And so on like that; his mother lost her job, they drove to San Francisco, et cetera. They always dealt with their grief elsewhere. Zack said he still had a Pavlovian response to traveling, fetching his suitcase with a reliably heavy heart for no apparent reason.

And how had my little family celebrated our disappointments? We were not so innovative. I remembered the oppressive loneliness of my mother's house when another good thing she'd hoped would happen didn't happen—the landscape architect, for instance; or the delicate insurance man with the mustache; the promotion at the leasing office they gave to young Patti Clem instead. So Mom and I played the radio and the TV at the same time and attended to neither with any interest. We stacked our dirty dishes high on the tables. We ate cereal for dinner and slept past breakfast.

Zack and I weren't wealthy and the trips we took had always been too small to call vacations. I'd lived with Zack in Portland for two years and still hadn't made it east of the Cascades. So we took off and spent two days in Hood River with Zack's sister and tacked on an extra night at an Airbnb in Maupin, just on the other side of the mountains for the first time. The Airbnb was cheap, and Zack's sister's house was free. Mel, Zack's sister, is easy—effortlessly warm, and treats me as an extension of her brother, with perfect fondness. Her home is prim and cottage-like and looks out on a bend in the Columbia where the kite surfers dangle on the wind over the river.

Our Airbnb in Maupin stood on the banks of the Deschutes River, smaller and more rustic than the Columbia, but beautiful, too. It sat in the middle of a high, mountain-rimmed pan of sagebrush desert in every direction: an attractive and old, one-story home in a heavy shade of cottonwoods with a gravel drive out front where a man was bent over futzing with a car cover. Typically, when traveling, we had avoided private rooms in occupied houses just to spare ourselves from making small talk with strangers on the way to the bathroom. We preferred the whole-home Airbnb rentals, where the hosts could remain remote and theoretical to us, and leave us free to pretend the host's furniture was our furniture, snoop through the empty cabinets, fool around in the kitchen, ridicule the wall art, and so on, but the place was cheap, as I said, and it was just the one night. However it should go, we'd have two bottles of wine and the river at the window.

The man futzing with the car told us where to park and then introduced himself as Wes who owned the house. He was an old man in his green shorts with a luxuriously full head of hair. "This is Melissa's show," he said. "She's just out of the shower. I know she'll like to meet you once she's pieced herself back together."

Wes started us on the tour without her. The home was an eccentric's hideout, absolutely full of colorful oddities. The walls were crowded with paintings and prints of paintings and folk art and photographs and refurbished trinkets of Americana and other more mysterious trinkets of the world. Funky instruments sat atop the wall-mounted cabinets, and the doors were each a different shade in pastels, the furniture mismatched and expensive. Wes waved his hand at this and that and said, "Well, I'll let Melissa give you the skinny on that." Books, too, lay everywhere. The corner room was shelved full of books, books piled on the floor, books piled precariously aslant on an old-fashioned music stand. Zack nudged me to note a stack of *New Yorkers* beside an armchair that stood almost as tall as the armrest, balancing a drink coaster on top. He raised a brow. We had not expected to find such diligent readers out in the middle of nowhere, although, we decided afterward, perhaps it's the most obvious place to find them.

We made it through three front rooms and past a little gated pantry where a big poodle and a tiny but otherwise identical poodle excited themselves to see us. Then Melissa met us with the dogs barking, in her silk robe and her wet hair, long and bleached, her eyes large with excitement behind her glasses. My first opinion of the woman: she seemed scattered and bohemian, old, but sexually aware. She smiled at Zack and me as though we had met for a secret rendezvous.

"Molly and Zack, it's so lovely to have you," she said. "Fresh faces, oh! Without even trying, I've learned the name of every face in Maupin and I'm tired of all of them. Has Wes given you a tour? What's he missed?" Then we started the tour over.

Melissa wanted to assure us she was not a hoarder, although her home was full of things that were semantically fairly close to trash. She had a shop online, she said, carefully curated items, knickknacks, heirlooms—here on a side table an old steel-pressed Coca-Cola sign, an antique coffee percolator, a lucha libre mask in a shadow box, and a postcard signed by Mia Farrow. "I've worked dozens of jobs in my life, but I am an artist first, then a collector," she said. "I learned to pick up hobbies that pay for themselves and sometimes a little extra."

I told her Zack tuned up old bicycles.

"It's a good excuse to buy more bikes than the regular guy," Zack said.

"Oh, simpatico!" Melissa clapped her hands. "Well, these are my bicycles, so to speak. I designed all you see in here," she said. "Wes was my engineer. That was his occupation back when. So I had him on the hook to get it put together for me, because I don't do math. I don't say, 'Make the counter eight feet and a quarter long and so-and-so high and the cabinets such and such higher.' I say, 'I want a honking slab of counter, pow, big like a farm table, big enough so that it says, hey you, sit with me, and I want a sink, also big, off-center at that end. I don't want any of it drawing the eye toward symmetrical thinking. When you're sitting in my kitchen, I want you to be in *my* kitchen, not in the *idea* of a kitchen. No autopilot allowed in my house.' And then Wes, he has such a handle on the way I think and talk, he just pencils in all the math and it comes out like, well——" She looked over the living room. "I say it comes out very handsomely. Wes is the know-how. I'm the inspiration."

"I'm also the cook," Wes said proudly.

"That's right. He's also the cook. And he's getting pretty good at that, too."

"There's the one little farmer's market in town," Wes said. Then he proceeded to give us very detailed directions, and we nodded along without paying attention. "Whatever they happen to got at that little market that day," Wes said, "that's what I'm learning to cook that night."

"When I turned sixty-five, I just said, no more cooking for me."

"No more cooking," Wes agreed.

"I decided I had zero interest in it. And Wes is getting pretty good. Still, sometimes he has an experiment that goes awry, but last week he made—what was that noodle one?"

"Pad kee mao."

"Right, and I'd never had a pad kee mao. Neither of us had. Maybe it had very little in common with whatever a pad kee mao is, but."

"But whatever it was, it was pretty good," Wes said.

"It's a beautiful home you have," I offered. "Wherever I look there's something to see."

"Like this big boy," Zack said, thumbing at a painting of a naked and massively overweight baby riding a terrier to apparent exhaustion.

"That's one of my son's," Melissa said.

"Riding the dog?" Zack asked.

"No, one of my son's paintings! Tell me, tell me," she said, "are you hip with the arts?"

"We pretend to be fashionable enough," Zack said.

"We're writers," I added, "if that counts."

"Well, Molly's a writer," Zack said. "I'm a hobbyist, but she's got a book coming out."

"I'm a writer myself!" Melissa said.

"Well," I said. "It goes to show you." Though I didn't know what it went to show at all or what I meant by it. I was talking in empty idioms just to bring myself closer to the end of the conversation, to our rented room, where I might seal myself away and feel human again.

"Tonight," Melissa said, "you'll have to take a glass of wine with us on the patio. I hope you will. I haven't had a chance to talk with writers since I lived in Georgia, and even my writer friends in Georgia, they were all poets and they were all secretly conservatives." Then she showed us her library again with renewed interest. We played the game where we pointed to books we've read or had been meaning to read. She spoke of her influences. I should say here that everyone, I believe, ought to write; the same as everyone ought to sing and dance and ruminate on the beauties of this life however comes naturally, but I'll add, at my peril, that I dread to meet an older lady with an idea for a memoir, or a talkative dude with his vision for a screenplay. In either case, after they've learned that I see myself as a writer-type, I'm never sure what is expected of me except to employ all my powers of active listening and my best impression of a bobblehead. It's like an acquaintance accosting you with a dream they had the night before, but it's a dream that had nothing to do with you.

The tour ended finally at the bedroom we'd sleep in. Melissa seemed to want to do it all over again. She stood in the bedroom doorway so that it couldn't be closed except very rudely in her face.

"And just so you know," Melissa said, tapping her nose, "you're young, maybe you smoke pot, and we don't judge you for that at all." Wes beside her studied his shoes.

"Oh, we've dabbled," Zack said. "But we've only brought this here." He held up our bottles of wine by the necks. I knew Zack did have pot, though, in his pack. Zack started smoking more pot to curb his drinking and now he liked to get stoned when he was buzzed.

"Well, it would have been all right if you did," Melissa said. "We smoke pot, too, on occasion. Not often out here anymore, because where would a couple old farts get it? No dispensaries this far from Portland."

"Right, sure," Zack said.

"So if you had any, we wouldn't mind at all if you wanted to make use of it. It's a very beautiful country out here—you can see that—but it's not very hospitable, I say, to open-minded people. We happen to be open-minded people. Even Wes—anywhere else he'd be a fuddy-duddy, but he's cutting-edge in this beautiful wasteland."

"Well, we just got the wine."

"I wanted to mention it," Melissa said. "This is why I do the Airbnb, you know."

"How's that?" I asked.

"Not for pot." She laughed. "For the social stimulation, I mean. The guests. For their stories of the world. It's beautiful, a beautiful country here, like I said, but the company, my God. For such a beautiful country, it hasn't attracted many tenants receptive to beauty."

ZACK WENT TO get our things from the car, and I hid in the bedroom. Another of Melissa's son's paintings hung on the wall above the bed, a chesty redhead on a midden of oyster shells. She was a strikingly robust woman, particular of face, and nude. On the dresser there were more knickknacks and folksy goods from indiscriminate countries—a little wooden devil man with a gargantuan penis, a ceramic turtle jar holding nothing, an old tin bread box holding nothing—and a neatly fanned stack of magazines, arranged before a row of books. Topping the pile there was an issue of *Central Oregon Design and Interior*. On its cover there was a house that seemed to be the house in which we stood, photographed in a greener season, with spears of lupine blooming in their purples. There was a bookmark in the magazine, marking a feature on—it certainly looked like—the home of Melissa and Wes, although their names were not mentioned in the article. The interior was more sparely decorated for the photoshoot, but it was unmistakably the house. The feature was called, "Paradise in the High Desert."

Melissa's was a larger room than Zack's sister had to offer, but it felt smaller for the busyness of the walls and crowded as it was with hardly usable furniture. We hadn't had any sex at Zack's sister's. Her guest room shared a wall with the master bedroom, and so Zack and I found ourselves whispering as though I'd snuck in through the window. The last trip we took, a year earlier, to the San Juan Islands in Washington, we stayed out late and drank until we felt like copies of ourselves. Then we went to bed like strangers. And since then, when Zack got drunk, he got it in his head that drunkenness was all we required to reproduce the San Juans in our apartment. But as it turned out, Melissa's guest room also shared a wall with the master bedroom, and offered just as little in the way of privacy. This was our first sexless vacation. I was relieved and too exhausted to let that worry me. So much of my energies then, it felt, were spent keeping Zack buoyed through his disappointments—thankless, unproductive work.

Zack finally managed to slip back into the room. I feared Melissa would sneak in under his arm, but he got the door closed behind him. I showed him the magazine I found.

"Of course she marked the page," he said. "Flagrant! Oh, hell, but it kind of makes me sad."

"What other goodies has she left for us?" I asked. The magazine waiting to be found, her son's painting on the wall. Desperate pleas to be known and thought well of by any old strangers. I looked through the books beside the magazines, pitying the woman, and at the end of the row, where it might be selected first, I saw a spine that read, *Praying for Sheetrock*, by a Melissa Fay Greene.

"You didn't catch our host's last name, did you?" I asked.

"No. Why?"

I held the book up. "Could it be . . . Fay Greene?"

"Oh, buzz off," Zack said, hopping over. I handed him the book. "No author photo," he said. "And I don't know the press. Maybe it's some sort of vanity press."

"Melissa is a common name," I said.

"Okay, I'm googling," he said, hunching over his phone. "And she's got a Wikipedia! Here: Melissa Fay Greene, born December 30, 1952—that might be about right actually, age-wise—is an American nonfiction author. A 1975 graduate of Oberlin College, Greene is the author of six books of nonfiction, a two-time National Book Award finalist!" Zack looked at me, astonished. "And a 2011 inductee into the Georgia Writers Hall of Fame. Georgia!" he repeated. "She said she was from Georgia, right? I remember Georgia."

"Let me see that."

"She has a bunch of books. Oh, but the picture. There's a picture of her. I don't know."

"Let me see," I said.

Well, it was a younger woman, maybe in her early forties, and our Melissa was now in her—I wasn't sure—mid-seventies. The author's hair, though, was rung in dark brown curls. I wasn't sure either way.

"Well, she'd be older now," Zack said.

"And her hair's bleached. The roots are dark anyway. It's hard to say what her natural hair might look like."

"Could she take the curl out?"

"Sure. People do," I said. And Melissa did seem like the sort of woman who was proclaiming herself transformed every year, then re-inventing her wardrobe to prove it.

Zack and I knew and cared very little about the literary non-fiction world and knew just as little about its celebrities. Still, we thought the abundance of literary magazines made more sense now. Who read the *New Yorker*, the *Paris Review*, *Harper's*, and all the like that lay about the living room, who wasn't a writer or who hadn't any aspirations of being one? Zack and I took inventory of Melissa's eccentricities and saw them illuminated now. How do you spot a crank's eccentricities from a genius's, anyway? Say, for instance, we theorized, all you knew about James Joyce was that he wrote lying in bed with large blue pencils? What if all you'd known of his writing were his fart-obsessed love letters? Would we have guessed him a crank or a genius then? Or what if all we knew of Flannery O'Connor was her racist correspondence and her massive collection of ground fowl? Or what about Capote, who never left more than three cigarette butts in the ashtray and tucked the surplus in his dirty pocket?

I'd had a neighbor once, years ago, who I thought of again as we constructed our notion of Melissa's genius. He was a middle-aged guy, divorced, who'd get drunk and start messing around with his bow and arrow. A few nights a week he was out there in his patio lights, shooting arrows into the trunk of a pine tree at the edge of his backyard. Daylight saw the tree brutalized and pitiful to look at, almost hilarious. One night when I was feeling talkative and lonesome, I called out to him. I said there had to be quicker ways to cut a tree down. He called back with surprising lucidity that he wasn't cutting anything down. He was an artist. He was making a self-portrait. And if that had been true, I might have thought of him, too, with more generosity, but all he produced by his art, as far as I could tell, was a tree full of arrows.

"No autopilot allowed in Melissa's house," Zack said. "That's like, maybe an asinine thing to say if you're an average joe, but if you're a

genius, maybe there's something more radical to it. Were we conde-
scending, do you think?"

"I think I looked bored," I said. "I couldn't help it."

"Imagine how I looked when she had me cornered in the hallway,"
Zack said. He was silent for a moment, running the conversation back
in his head with a wince. "I told her I really had to get to the bathroom."

ON MELISSA'S RECOMMENDATION, we went to dinner at a place called
Ramble's, a little brewhouse and lodge at the river on the lawn where
the rafters put in. Zack and I sat outside and ordered our meal, and
then he took Melissa's book from his bag with a little flourish and
read me the first page. I was surprised and glad that he'd brought the
book. Was the book good? I supposed it was. Judging by the first page
and Zack's tone, I supposed it was very good in that way that almost
everything you want to be good seems very good. A Labrador visited
our table, and Zack absently handed the dog french fries as he read,
until the dog's owner kindly asked him to stop.

"She's good, isn't she?" Zack said and waited for me to agree. The
dog continued to sit at his knee. Zack was happy to find us both en-
thused about the same thing for the first time in a while. "I mean, if it's
her, then she's good, isn't she? It's nonfiction, but it's novelistic."

Melissa had asked us, in the library portion of the tour, to see our
writing. Or she wanted to know if we had websites she could peruse.
We had politely brushed this off with false humility and genuine disin-
terest, and Zack was smarting about it now. "It's always kind," he said,
"don't get me wrong—it's always a kind gesture when anyone wants

to see your work, but when it's like a National Book Award–caliber writer, who's asking to read your work, well. That's uncommon, isn't it? Who gets the National Book Award and then offers to read some unknown writer's work?"

"National Book Award nominee," I said.

"Right," Zack said. "A two-time nominee."

"If it's her at all," I said.

"Right, but if it is her, you just wouldn't expect that, would you?"

"Which part?" I asked.

"Maybe she'll blurb your book," Zack said. "If she asks to see our writing again, I could send her my story about the horse-trailer crash. Is that bad?"

"Not if she asks," I said.

"Right. Exactly."

Zack and I hadn't spoken this easily and with such enthusiasm, on his part, about the business of writing for some time. The promising things happening for me only underscored the promising things that weren't happening for him, and it became increasingly easy for him to interpret a good thing that didn't happen, inversely, as a bad thing that did happen. That frightened me, and how the subject chafed his spirits. He was drinking more, and I pretended not to notice. He was starting a new story every week and throwing it out, feeling each time as though he were about to be left behind at the station. In the meantime, he took on more responsibilities at the bike shop and neglected his facial hair. I worried it might undo us if things kept on like that. Already I'd begun looking forward to my bad news, just to share it with Zack—like writing thirty pages in the wrong direction only to scrap it all, or a fresh rejection, an editor's harsh critique, a canceled reading—just to see him soften again. I often came home to find him pretending to be sober in front of the TV, and oh, I think, my poor man, your head down in your hands, so miserable in your favorite shoes.

WE WERE FULL and we had a couple drinks apiece and the light was going golden in the air. Zack and I, like anyone else, are both better at loving each other when we don't feel rotten about ourselves. We watched a family get up to leave and another family take their place. He looked at me and smiled. I said we should return and find the pair of bicycles Melissa and Wes had mentioned in their Airbnb posting and take a ride up the river. Zack agreed, but said he'd also like to see what Melissa and Wes were doing first, which happened to be sitting out on the screened-in porch watching the river go by. Melissa asked us how Ramble's was, and we said pretty good. She told us pretty good was about as much as you could hope for in Maupin.

"What about a glass of wine," Zack said, to my surprise and displeasure. "Is that still in the cards?"

So we drank a bottle of their wine. It was evening. There was still some heat in the sunlight, and from where we sat on the porch, I watched a gathering of cattle in the neighboring plot shade themselves beneath the long, slanting shadow of a juniper tree. We finished the first bottle between the four of us and we uncorked a second Zack had retrieved from the room, and then Zack told Melissa he had to come clean about something. God help me, I thought. He's arriving at the book.

"Oh?" she said.

"Here's the thing," Zack said. "Actually, we do have pot."

"Oh?" she said again in much the same tone.

"It's just that my first instinct, when someone asks about pot, is to lie. It makes me back into a teenager. It's like you said. I wasn't sure how hospitable this place is to open-mindedness."

"And you've concluded we're not the secret police after all?"

"I hope you won't disappoint me, Melissa." Then he handed her a THC pen from his pocket and showed her how to use it. Soon we were stoned in addition to the wine buzz, all of us, including Wes, who'd now grown very interested in the workings of his hands. Melissa wanted to make something clear to me about the river. "Oh, rivers," she said. "They have no names for themselves, do they, but for Babble Babble? They introduce themselves ceaselessly, ceaselessly." Zack, for his part, was trying to steer the conversation to books.

"With a library like yours," he said, "and porch like this, you could really read all the day long out here."

"It's only the river that makes me feel human in this town," she said.

On the end table between Melissa and me there was a photo of a redheaded woman on a barstool. I wrestled with the feeling of vaguely recognizing her face before I remembered the painting in the bedroom of the redheaded nude. This was a photograph of a real woman of course, and not a painting, so her tits weren't out, but I saw it was the same woman. I was sure it was. I asked Melissa if I was right.

"She's all over this place, isn't she," Melissa said. I had the feeling she'd been waiting for me to notice. "That's our Eva. That's Wes's first wife. The painting in the bedroom, I commissioned that one from my son." Zack and I looked at the picture together and saw the redheaded woman and knew she was dead.

"She's beautiful," Zack said, then he looked at me as if he didn't know where that had come from.

"Yes," Melissa said. "Wasn't she. Well, Wes and I are about as old as we look, and we've both outlived our first spouses years ago now. Rest in peace."

I mumbled my sympathies to the photograph of the redheaded Eva. Suddenly I felt very high. I didn't like it. I didn't want to be there, pretending not to be very high. Even the birds seemed to notice how high I was, all of them turning their dark little heads to watch me. Melissa laughed inscrutably.

"No, no, I'm being a rascal; my first husband, he isn't *dead* dead. He's just dead to me." She laughed again. "Oh, I don't mean that exactly either, do I! He's fine, but I have a few expectedly ugly feelings about him and how I was with him. Wes's first wife, on the other hand—Eva is quite passed away, and we treat her like something of a saint in this house. There's at least one likeness of her in every room. I never got to meet the woman, but I've laid flowers on her grave and I have made love to the last man she made love to, and I say that's about as close as one could come to meeting her now."

"Maybe the only man she ever made love to," Wes said. "I miss my old wife and I am thankful for my new wife. Some people want to see a conflict between those two notions, but there isn't one."

"I'll admit, I was a bit boneheaded on the subject," Melissa said conspiratorially. "Only at the outset, though. But then, on our eighth anniversary, I sent Wes into town for the day and when he got back, I had her pictures up in every room, even the bathrooms. That was my idea. Wes cried like a baby."

"For about a week I did," Wes said. He laughed. "I couldn't set foot in any room without crying. I'd leave her picture in one room and then I'd see her picture in the next room and I'd start up all over again."

Melissa picked the photo up without much interest and then set it down, shrugging. "And it's true, of course, if you live long enough, there's just no holding on to your saintliness. If she'd lived to my age, who's to say if she and Wes might have belittled each other over the dinner table like the rest of us? But of course I don't like to get into hypotheticals. What's the point? Let her be preserved in all her youth and beauty forever and ever. Why not? Leave her that much because, my God, what else does she have?"

"If I met her again today," Wes said, "just as old as she was when she passed, she'd seem like a child to me. And I'd be an old man to her."

I was embarrassed to see that Wes was crying softly beside me. Zack stared at Melissa for a moment, nodding as he, it seemed, formed a thoughtful opinion. "Melissa," he said. "Do you read much short fiction?"

Melissa did, of course. She and Zack traded their favorite short story writers back and forth without any overlap or any loss of enthusiasm for it. Meanwhile, Wes sat there beside them time-traveling misty-eyed through the private joys of his life, which existed, I understood, without corroboration now, in his memory alone, as fragile and unsubstantiated as a dream. My attentions were split: Wes, having a moment at my one side, and on the other I hear Zack telling Melissa about his rejections, making the unspeakable thing shockingly speakable.

"Now I'm wondering if I can bear it," he said, "to throw this book out, four years of my life out, and if I do, if I could bear that much, could I ever bear to try again?"

"Listen now, Zack," Melissa said. "I've been told to go home count-less times in my life, God knows. But you can't. You've got to get back inside to the party. You've got to get back to the bar and buy a pretty girl a drink!"

Zack laughed and nodded woefully. As a means, I thought, of en-couragement, Melissa asked Zack what he wrote about.

"Oh, I hate to talk about my work," he said, raising himself at the edge of his seat. "But it's kind of you to ask. If I had to try: the man-uscript I'm sitting on is largely an interrogation of archetypal mascu-linity." He'd earlier auditioned *toxic masculinity* as his pitch phrase, but I guessed the mounting social purchase of *toxic masculinity* had begun to dissuade him. He might as well have said, guys doing guy stuff with unproductive gestures of self-reflection. "And addiction, too, that's the other thing," he said. "Addiction, masculinity—they've got this interplay going. But I don't want to have too much fun with it, the way a lot of writers have, the romanticization of getting fucked-up. You know? I don't want any more hallucinatory drug sequences like out of some nineties music video. It's a different world these days, more urgent. There's kids I grew up with we've stuck in the ground from overdoses. Christ, there are people of color being killed in the streets, you know? The last thing we need is another book about white guys, dangling themselves over their safety nets, entertaining masturbatory fantasies of self-destruction."

Melissa nodded along with enthusiasm, even adoration. "Oh yes," she said, and, "Mhmm, mhmm," and, "Right, how right, what a lovely way to say it."

Writers are a needy, helpless lot. Give them a few compliments and they're yours for life. I should add, though, that I adored Zack's work. It's what touched me about him from the start. We had encountered each other a number of times over the years at readings and writers' conferences and other literary events we purported to hate but attended anyway. We both lived in Baltimore for a couple overlapping years. There were good stretches of time in between our encounters, too. Just long enough to forget the other almost completely. At another conference in Minneapolis—I'd since moved to Atlanta, and he'd since moved to Portland, where he'd grown up—we found ourselves shoulder to shoulder at the hotel bar. He'd often been fairly drunk at these things, and I didn't guess he remembered my name, so I told him again and he told me his and then he said, "One of these days, Molly, we've got to stop introducing ourselves."

He was a goofy, amicable young guy playing the fool, handsome in his silly shirts, great fun for a brash night, but I wondered about substance. His work, though—truly it is thoughtful work—said to me, maybe there's more to this idea. It's true, his women characters these days often said things I recall saying myself. I've seen a few of my own happy memories recast in his tragedies, some of my tragedies in his comedies. And just the same, I've found his phrases written into my work, too. We had each other's voices coming out of our mouths. There are those couples you know that married right out of high school, and after ten years of eating the same meals they've begun to look like siblings: that's where we were headed.

"But really we should be talking about Molly's book," Zack said, seeing I was elsewhere in my head. "She's the one about to catch a meteoric rise."

"Is that right? You'll have to write the title down for me so I can find a copy."

"Please, don't listen to him," I said.

"It's true," Zack said. "Molly's book is hitting the shelves next year. It's going to be one of those books people actually read. No, I really believe that. Me, I'll still be working at the bike shop, but I'll be able to say I knew Molly back when."

"He's joking," I said. I felt myself getting irritated, getting cold in my irritation. If Zack praised me, in those days, it was almost always in service to his self-deprecation. "Please, Melissa, tell us what you write about."

The question delighted Melissa. She was a journalist, she said, on and off in her life, and that's where she was most comfortable. "Mostly, I write essays, but I wish I could write fiction like you two. I've tried my hand and all my efforts stunk up the room."

"I doubt that. I really doubt that," Zack said.

"Well, we'll see. I'm trying again, actually, for no defensible reason. I have no idea if the thing's any good, but I keep coming back to it."

"Well, I'm already positive it's good," Zack said. "I'd put money on it. All you need is to hear someone else say it."

Melissa turned to me and said, "Oh, I like this one. I expect he's quite a cheerleader for you."

"You should let me read it," Zack said. "I don't have anything in the way of pedigree like the two of you, but I'm a sharp editor. Molly, I'm a sharp editor, aren't I?"

"I couldn't ask you to do that," Melissa said. Zack told her that he was the one asking. Well, then, Melissa said, she had one condition. "You'll have to send me your book. We'll call it a trade."

I had never witnessed Zack work a conversation like this before, but then I'd never known him as desperate as he was now. Melissa and

Zack spoke on with the shared elation of new lovers, about books and writing, eventually lifting themselves from the sofa and floating on that elation down the hall back to the library, where Melissa had a few books she wanted to lend Zack. I didn't follow them, and they didn't seem to mind. I wondered if one might try to kiss the other.

Wes noticed only sometime after the fact that only he and I remained. He looked at me and he smiled. It was a kind, generous smile, broad and bemused. It said to me, "Well, look at us all. Look at us four strangers sharing one evening. Life has happened to us by accident, Molly. Everything was all a roll of the dice."

"Well, I'm stoned off my butt," he said.

"Me too," I said.

"I think I'll go to bed now."

"Okay, Wes."

"Good night. Forgive me. I don't remember your name. Good night." Then, I'm sure he got up and wandered down the hall, but as I remember it, I blinked and he vanished.

I was alone then, studying the walls, a traffic collision of colors, Melissa's mind and personality externalized onto the poor house. Shouldn't it be beautiful, then—the manifestation of her interior life, of any interior life? Or should it have made me squeamish the way it did? I saw another stack of *New Yorkers* at my side. The mailing label on the cover was addressed to a Melissa Stahancyk. I picked the magazine up and looked at the address more carefully. An odd cudgel of a name, I thought.

Zack returned with a book in either hand and one under his arm as Melissa made a stop at the kitchen for a glass of water. I held the magazine out to Zack, bearing Melissa's real name, which he took happily and set on the table without inspection.

"You'll have to give me your address, Melissa," he said. "I don't think I'll finish these tonight. I'll have to mail them to you."

Melissa returned from the kitchen before I could impress my discovery upon Zack. She asked how we managed to get to the house in the first place without an address.

"Oh, right," Zack said. He laughed.

"And you just hold on to them anyway."

"No way," Zack said. "I couldn't."

"Sure, sure." Melissa shooed away the thought. "Keep them. I hope you connect with them."

"I'm sure I will. And with your novel, too. That's really what I'm looking forward to. I've got my reading for the rest of the summer all accounted for now."

"Well, if you do," Melissa said. She sat down and steadied herself in her seat. "If you really think it's any good, my novel, maybe you could send it along to your agent? Or maybe you could put me in contact with someone. How did you go about meeting your agent?"

I saw here what was about to happen, and I already believed it was my fault, not just because I hadn't done everything in my power to avert it, but because secretly, in my heart, there was a dark kernel of malice that wished for it, one glancing bolt of a resentment. I might have stood and waved my arms, pretended I was bitten by an invisible bug, thrown up in my lap, threatened to piss my pants, or interrupted the conversation in any number of ways, but I didn't.

"My agent, what for?" Zack asked.

"Oh God, I'm being crass, aren't I?"

"But what about your agent?"

"Who?"

"Did you part ways, or?"

"I've never had an agent."

"But your book," he said. "How else did you sell *Praying for Sheet-rock?*"

"I'm sorry?"

"We saw it in the bedroom."

"I haven't read it, I'm afraid."

By this point I saw that Zack understood, but he wasn't ready to give himself over to understanding. "*Praying for Sheetrock,*" he said, "Melissa Fay Greene," as if it might change her mind.

"Oh," she said.

We sat with this revelation. The merriness of the night evaporated from under us and left us three adults in a room of expensive trash. Melissa was blinking insanely as she made sense of the situation.

"It's very late, isn't it? It's very late, and I think I'm embarrassing myself."

She stood and told us again to help ourselves to the fridge and where to find the light switches and then she hurried down the hall.

We went to bed too, without saying anything else to each other. Later I would understand that this was only one of the many nights of our lives, and it wouldn't change much of anything, but it was dark, it was a stranger's house, and we were high and ashamed of ourselves, and everything loomed over us catastrophically. We used the bathroom in turns in silence. The guest bed was massive, and we lay on exceptional pillows with a gulf of bedsheets between us. If I didn't say something kind to this man before we fell asleep, I thought we might wake up as strangers. It has happened before. For a long time, I thought about this and then I fell asleep.

* * *

IT WAS MORE than a week after we'd arrived back home to our lives in Portland that Melissa emailed Zack with her novel manuscript. He laughed when he saw it turn up in his inbox, but when I asked what it was, he was solemn. That Melissa had waited on the email this long said to me: she told herself she would not send her manuscript after all, but then, after a week sitting with it, something got the better of her. The manuscript was three hundred and thirty-seven pages. She called it *Trespassers in the Country of God.*

Zack asked me if I wanted to hear the first paragraph, but I didn't. I wished he hadn't told me any of it, really—that he'd received the manuscript at all, or that in her email, Melissa wrote gracious things about an interview of mine she'd found online. I didn't care to learn any more about my condescensions. Zack read the manuscript on his own. He spent the next week working through the first half, going slowly, marking the margins with generous notes, compliments, suggestions for revision. It surprised me. He worked late each night and told me nothing about the book except for how many pages he'd read.

Now that we were home again, Zack resumed checking his email for any news from his agent, but not with the previous week's urgency. There were just a few more names on Zack's list of manuscript submissions, none of which would pan out in the end. The bad news was coming, and we might have guessed it already, but Zack continued to read Melissa's book with diligence. The only thing I knew about Melissa's book was that it made Zack kinder to himself as he worked his way through it, scratching his jaw and making his notes. And suddenly we were waking without fear in the mornings, reading each other passages of novels over our coffee. We tried to teach ourselves to play tennis in the evenings without bothering to keep score or look up the rules. I thought, all our weeks couldn't be this pleasant, could they, but what a good week it was shaping up to be. We called our friends just to say we were thinking of them and watched TV without guilt. One morning he stepped out for a jog and kissed me through the windowpane, making a smudge of his face on the glass that remained for months until I finally sprayed it with cleaner. That was our week of kindness, perfect by any measure except that it would end.

Zack never managed to finish reading Melissa's book. He is still meaning to get back to it. Occasionally we'll be out and about and her book, where it's buried in his inbox, occurs to him again with a shock of guilt. Last time he told me, "I'll just have to write her the letter of her life, then. I'll tell her everything she's ever wanted to hear. A letter so magnificent that she'll hardly remember how long it took me to send it."

THE DROWNED WOMAN

L ATE IN THE summer, Charlie saw something floating in the reservoir. He called Sam over from the pile of wood he had been arranging into the firepit and they stood together for a moment and watched the black water, the shape in it, which was not moving. Beneath them the thick muck shore glistened in the moonlight and extended back into the brush and there were a few fallen trees and apple-sized stones scattered around. Even here, twenty-some miles from the nearest town, there was garbage. There was a torn grocery bag in the limb of a split-backed juniper, and a broken sandal on a rock, and half a beer bottle beneath that with the label washed off. The moon was both in the sky and reflected in the lake.

"That's not a log, is it?" Charlie said.

"No, I don't think it is."

"That's a person. It is, isn't it?"

"Maybe it is."

"Couldn't be alive, you think?"

"No. I don't think so."

Charlie called out to the shape and asked if it was alive. He threw a handful of mud out into the water, which broke apart into ripples and took apart the vision of the moon and did not stir the facedown shape.

Sam looked out behind them at the dirt trail, which led to the decommissioned turbine house where the men had been sleeping. The walls were mostly whole still, but doorless, and the corrugated roof had collapsed in some areas where stones had fallen from the overhang above. In other areas the roof was bent and holding rocks and threatening to collapse at any moment, perhaps at night as Charlie slept right beneath it, straight upon him, cracking his head open, sending him from one dark to the other without his knowing. He thought about this sometimes, but the worry was not enough to keep him awake. The men slept curled around paint-chipped turbines and gears and stale rubber machine belts that had split and littered the place with black splinters of rubber.

Some distance beyond the turbine house there was a car only hardly visible through the trees. They might not have noticed it before morning if they hadn't seen the figure in the water. Sam turned back to Charlie, who was watching the figure carefully, flicking his fingers with his thumb.

Sam said, "That car probably belonged to it in the water."

"What do we do?"

"About what?"

"Could still be alive."

"It's not alive."

"Go check," Charlie said.

"You go. I already know what I'll find."

"I can't. My foot. I'm still drying out the infection."

"The car must have belonged to it there in the water."

"Maybe it's alive."

"Couldn't be alive."

"Would you go on and check, Sam?"

"What for?"

"If it were me, I'd like for someone to give a damn, even if I was dead. I'd like for someone to check anyway. Just to know."

"No one would give a damn, Charlie."

"Well, that's what I'd want."

So Charlie sat on the stump and pulled his boots off and his socks, one of which had fused to his misshapen foot. He hung them from a low tree branch.

"Christ. The stink, Charlie," Sam said. "The stink of it."

"I know," he said, and eased his foot down into the coolness of the mud and felt it soak into his split skin. The pain was more distinct every day. It was as though his body were waking up to another world, which was more real, and more painful. The feeling of it oscillated between aches, low and warm, and lances of white agony. Walking on it was possible, but only barely, and then there was the feeling that this possibility was nearing the edge of itself. And after that? He imagined he'd have a long time to sit and think about this when it happened that he could no longer stand. Charlie and Sam did not discuss eventualities. They had always kept to the thing at hand.

Charlie waded out waist-deep and found that the shape was a woman, and the woman was dead. Charlie called out to Sam, "A lady." The dead woman turned over effortlessly in his arms in the water. He held his ear to her lips and didn't hear anything. Charlie hadn't touched a woman in a very long time.

"Dead?" Sam asked.

"Yeah."

"I said so."

"She's a pretty one, Sam," he said. Her hair was dark and smooth and galvanized with silver bands of moonlight. Her skin was nearly without color except for a faint purple beneath her eyes and at the corners of her mouth. She was wearing jeans, and a sweater floated loosely about her torso in the water—which was trim and built as though to cradle a pair of hands, there at the hips. There was a haunted beauty in her face, which came to him like a lullaby from an open window. Her eyes were open. Sam yelled at him to leave her, but Charlie took her anyway beneath the arms and towed her back to shore.

"Can't leave her out here to sink."

"It's as good a place as any."

"Not here in the algae and the weeds. She'll fall apart."

"That's how it happens anywhere, Charlie."

He pulled her ashore until her feet were just above the waterline. Charlie knelt down beside her and Sam followed.

"You're right," Sam said. "She is a pretty one."

"Where do you figure her shoes went?" Charlie said.

Sam considered her feet for a moment and then he said, "Car must be hers. She must have walked right by us while we slept." Charlie moved the strands of hair from her face and Sam patted her front jeans pockets, and then he pushed his hands beneath her to go through her back pockets, which made Charlie wince. "No wallet. But here—" Sam removed his knuckles from her pocket with some difficulty. "Here we are." He held a key chain out in his palm. "Must be her car out back."

"Must be."

Sam looked down at her bare feet, traversed the length of her body, pausing over a pale strip of midriff. He ran his thumb over the nub of her hip.

"Hell, Sam," Charlie said. "Cut it out."

"Cold, isn't she?"

"I'm serious, Sam. Cut it out."

"All right," he said.

Sam left to find the car and Charlie stayed for a few moments and looked at the woman and wondered how long she'd been dead. He struggled with his socks and his boots and was unable to fit the second boot back over his infected foot because it was swollen and because it hurt and because he worried he might pull it apart. He left the boot and instead put the foot into a plastic grocery bag and tied it off around the ankle.

He found Sam in the driver's seat of an old Volvo, rummaging through the glove compartment. The forest and Charlie and everything else was hidden in the dark, and Sam glowed in the car's yellow, interior light. "No wallet here either," Sam said. "Registration, though. Car belonged to an Evelyn Barnard. Figure that was her in the water."

Through the tinted windows Charlie saw a child's safety seat illuminated by the light above the center console.

"You didn't see a kid out there in the water, did you?" Charlie asked.

"Why?"

"Kiddie seat back here."

Sam looked back for a moment and said, "Go figure."

"Think she was a mother?"

"Appears so," he said as he rifled through the center console, finding only a pack of tissues, a comb, and a travel-size bottle of hand moisturizer. He knocked down the visor and knocked it back up.

"I don't get it," Charlie said. "What was a mother doing out here in the dark?"

"It's a quiet place for it."

"For what?"

"Come on."

"I don't think that's it," Charlie said. "Something else must have happened."

"Mothers kill themselves too."

"She doesn't look the sort."

"My grandmother," Sam said, "she took the family car out into the fields with a little grill in the back seat. Suffocated herself with the fumes. That's how they found her. Didn't matter that she was somebody's mother." Sam wrenched around and went through the pockets at the back of the seats. "And how would you know anyway what sort she was?"

"Should we be rifling through the car, Sam?"

"Nobody's car anymore."

"We ought to tell someone about her."

"Who?"

"Somebody'll be looking for her. Somebody will wonder where she's gone."

"Guess we could drive the car into the city. Tell the police."

Charlie backed away from the car a ways, hobbling. "I don't know," he said. "Doesn't seem right, driving her car. Feels like stealing."

"We've stolen before."

"Not like this we haven't."

Sam gave up searching and stepped out and made for the trunk. "All right, Charlie. How then? We shout until a hiker hears us?"

"I don't know."

There was nothing in the trunk except a pair of sandals and an empty water bottle.

Sam stood back with Charlie for a moment and looked the car over and jostled the keys in his palm absently. "We'll have to drive it in to Estacada. Let them know we found her."

"I don't feel right getting in that car, Sam."

"I don't see the difference it makes."

Charlie shrugged and turned away from the conversation to think.

"I can go on my own," Sam said. "Bring a ranger back with me."

Charlie didn't say anything. He studied the key in Sam's hand and did not look at his face. "You drive up in a dead woman's car, they might suspect you for a murderer."

"No one's gonna suspect me for no murderer."

Sam waited for Charlie to protest again or change his mind and when Charlie did neither, Sam got in the car and twisted the key in the ignition and idled there a moment. He rolled down the window. "You can just wait here," he said. And then he drove off. The red glow of the taillights dissolved into the forest and the sound too of the car and of the gravel beneath the tires. It went quiet, and there were only the lonely noises of the trees and the nighttime and a bird somewhere hooting.

Charlie sat on a rock some yards away from the woman and watched her lying there. He saw the stillness in her chest and the lifeless angles of her feet and her fingers. It was cold out and the fire was dying. Sam would not be happy about it, but Charlie decided anyway that it would be best to take her inside the turbine house to protect her from the elements. Charlie was once able to carry a woman in his arms, but not anymore. She was too heavy for him and his hurt foot, and she was ragdoll limp, so he couldn't get the right hold on her. He knelt in the mud beside her and tried to rock her up into his grip. He slipped his arms beneath her back and beneath her thighs. Her head tossed around in the effort, lolling about on her little birdlike neck, so he gave up and caught his breath and apologized to the woman. He took her beneath the arms and dragged her over the threshold of the old stone room and laid her down in a corner where the roof still held.

"This'll be better in here," he said.

Charlie set up that night on the opposite corner of the room beneath a hole in the roof, beneath a small and starless cutout of overcast sky, and he fell asleep thinking about her name—Evelyn Barnard—and how it seemed to suit her somehow.

IN THE MORNING Charlie remembered her and found that she was still there and saw her for the first time in the daylight. Her hair had dried some and was auburn now, and her mouth was slack and half-open. Open eyes. My Lord. It was as though she were about to say something or to ask what became of her. Charlie was sorry for her. He felt guilty for looking at her so shamelessly when she hadn't the ability to turn away or to adjust her shirt over her white, crescent slip of midriff. He stepped outside.

Charlie, with tremendous effort, walked the shore, watching for stray fishhooks and bottle pieces. He paused occasionally to rest his foot and to watch the water exhale wisps of steam into the morning light. There was a bark-stripped pine limb between the rocks, which Charlie took as a walking stick. He didn't notice the smell of the place anymore—of the water, the fish in it, and the algae and the wet dirt and the tree needles. Ahead there was a creek that entered the reservoir, which was where Charlie and Sam cast the wire crawdad pot. Charlie picked up the nylon towline and hauled it in and felt the cage trundle along the stone bottom. He found four of them there—four copper-brown and buggy bodies. One crawdad was half-formed and missing a claw. As he plucked them up with his fingers, just at the start of the tail, they arched back and opened and closed their claws and tried to catch hold of him. He set them in his jacket pockets and threw the pot back midway into the creek and walked back with the muddy crustaceans pulsing dully against him.

Charlie started the fire and put a pot of water on that, then lowered the crawdads into the hot crackle of it where they clicked about for a while and died and turned a pretty shade of red. Charlie set two aside for Sam and cracked the tails open of the remaining pair and sucked the meat from the claws, then crushed what was left into chum, which he'd bait the crawdad pot with. He poured a tin mug of still-warm crawdad water and sipped on that, leaning against the wall of the turbine shack. These were the necessities of life, and for a while he had made do, except there was now a woman behind the wall, which made Charlie feel both more and less alone all at once.

The afternoon wore on and the shadows of the trees receded. Charlie watched the road. Sunlight fell through the forest in heavy slabs. Sam needed perhaps only a few hours to reach Estacada and relate the news and to return. It had been longer than that. Charlie thought maybe it was the precinct. Maybe they'd figured out who the car belonged to and took it off Sam's hands. It was possible, Charlie knew, that Sam had not gone into town at all. The two men had already stayed at the reservoir longer than they'd expected to. By Charlie's count, this would be his thirteenth night in the turbine house. They had meant to make it to the coast. Sam said he still knew a few names in Lincoln City. He might have just pressed on. Maybe he was already a hundred miles away, opting to keep the car, opting to keep his future ahead of him.

Sam didn't return that night. The firelight did little against the coming dark—and then the wholeness of it—the height of the forest blocking out the small light of the moon and the stars.

Late in the night it rained hard. Turned the firepit ash to black mud. Heavy raindrops panged against the metal roof and collected in the corrugated grooves and ran down into the shack in dark ribbons. Charlie woke to it and pulled up his blankets and his padding and stood for a moment under cover. The room wasn't large and felt even smaller for the rows of turbines and forgotten machinery. All that was left was the space next to the woman and the wall. So Charlie lay there next to her. This is how he and Sam had slept too in the wet cold. They lay like this and matched the patterns of their breathing and fell asleep, waking each other some nights with soft sleep-talking pleas for forgiveness. Charlie adjusted himself deep into his bundle of blankets and caught the woman with his elbow. The quiet of the place was beaten up by the metallic pitter-patter above them.

There was a smell in the room. The smell was faint enough still, but it was with them. Something spoiled. Charlie knew the smell may be her—there was every few hours a more distinct hollowness to her cheeks, and clouds in her eyes, a color in her skin—but then he thought perhaps the smell was him, too. There was the bag over his foot, though it had small holes enough to let some amount of water in and some sick out. His foot was hot, and the bag was thick with moisture, and he remembered vaguely how it had looked uncovered in the dark. He was afraid to inspect it in the daylight anymore. The smell of rot was on them both.

It wasn't just rancid. It was that too—that was what lingered afterward in Charlie's nostrils—but there was a sweetness beneath it, which reminded him of something he couldn't recall. The memory was gone but there was the place where the memory used to be, and there was something Charlie recognized in the shape.

IN THE MORNING Charlie ate the two crawdads he'd saved for Sam and recast the crawdad pot and later stood in the doorway to the shack, leaning against what little was left of the wooden doorframe. He did not want to imagine she'd meant to die. He thought about the child seat in the car.

Sam had not returned. Charlie tied a second bag over his foot since the first had begun to tear, and then he followed the old fire road up a ways, up through the first curves along the hillside. It led only to the lake, not through to anywhere. He tried to ignore his pain. In the noon hour the mounting heat dulled his focus. Occasionally a stick seemed to leap before his shuffling feet and transform itself into a grasshopper.

Charlie went on until he reached the pair of crosses at the shoulder. There was, on each, a wire ring hung at the joint, which had been strung once with a wreath of flowers, or paper hearts, or handwritten affirmations of love. One cross slouched crookedly. Charlie hammered it into the gravel with a flat stone and he looked at them a moment—at their twin shadows—and then he turned and began walking back to camp. For the first time, it felt as though there were only so many footsteps left in him, and that each was one forever expended. He had not planned to return home, back up the chimney of Idaho, but now he could not anyway. This was it. This was the extent—these hills, these shores, these the exact bounds of human existences, so far as he was concerned.

Night came again and the rain with it. Charlie returned to the dead woman's corner and settled beneath the blankets beside her. The smell of decay was there with them, and it was stronger now. He breathed a while through a mildewed blanket because it worried him to breath the smell of her, but he slipped soon enough into half sleep and let the blanket slip. The scent followed him into his dreaming. He traced through to the sweetness of it. Peeled through the layers of it, down to the heart.

IN THE MORNING there was the sound of a car, and then the sound of car doors opening and closing. In their time so far at the reservoir, Charlie and Sam had seen no human traffic, unless, Charlie thought, you counted the woman. He left her and stood out by the firepit with a blanket shawled around his shoulders. It wasn't Sam who had come, and it wasn't the ranger. A man came down the path with his kid son beside him holding a fishing rod. When the man saw Charlie standing there he stopped, and the kid saw this and stopped too. The man surveyed the camp.

"Morning," he said.

Charlie nodded. "Morning."

"You set up here?"

Charlie looked around, at the few pots and a plastic bucket and his boot still upright in the dirt. "Yeah."

"You've got the view." He gestured to the water and the opposite shore.

Charlie nodded.

The boy studied the turbine house behind Charlie and edged out a ways and leaned his head to the side. Charlie stepped back a few paces and rested in the doorway.

"What's in there?" the kid asked. His father put a hand down on his shoulder.

Charlie said, "Nothing. Just where I've set up."

"What's it for?" the kid asked.

"Nothing anymore. Just for sleeping."

"You live here?" the boy asked incredulously.

The man slung his hand down across his kid's chest and pulled him back a step. "He's camping out, bud. We've camped out."

"That's right," Charlie said.

"We use a tent," the kid said.

And the father told him, "This works too." He thought a moment and watched Charlie. And then he said, "Much to catch out there?"

Charlie looked down at the reservoir. "Crappies mostly. Some trout."

"Is your foot okay?" the kid said.

"Just a bit swollen is all."

"Is that your shoe over there?"

"That's it."

"Come on," the man said, "let's go try our luck."

The kid trotted off and walked backward for a ways to see if he couldn't catch a glimpse into the turbine house, but Charlie made sure he couldn't. The man studied Charlie cautiously for a moment. He had the look of someone about to say something, but then he smiled curtly and nodded and followed his kid to the water.

For a couple hours the father and son stood out there fishing, and for a couple hours Charlie sat against the turbine house and watched them. A few times the boy tangled his line around the rod or hooked it on a drowned tree and the father stooped with his pliers and righted it. At first Charlie wished that they'd move on soon, but after a while he relaxed and listened to their voices travel out across the water in soft echoes. He saw low-flying birds chase their reflections over the lake and plunge into the woods.

Then the kid went hip hollering and Charlie could see the rod buckle over and he heard the father shouting out instructions. What they pulled from the water, he could see from this distance, was a rainbow trout. He saw the color catch the sunlight, throwing off sharp glances of ruby and green. The father and the son marveled at the fish for a while. The boy ran his fingers down the wet, shimmering body. They looked back at Charlie and held up the fish for him to see.

They walked back to the camp, the father holding the rod and the kid holding the line and the fish hanging from it. The three of them looked at the fish in silence and agreed in that way that the fish was good. It was the best-looking trout Charlie had ever seen. The father nodded to his kid.

"Here," the kid said to Charlie. "Have it."

Charlie thought about this and said, "That's your catch. Trout's a good fish."

"We normally catch and release," the man said. "My wife's back home. Probably got the meal ready. So go on. Or we'll turn it loose."

"All right," Charlie said.

"You got someplace to put it?"

Charlie gestured to the bucket.

"RJ," the man said to his son, "why don't you go fill that bucket with water."

"How much?"

"Doesn't matter."

The kid handed the line and the fish to Charlie and then ran off with the bucket. The metal handle had cracked off in some past life, so the kid held it in his arms against his chest. Charlie watched the kid go and felt the man watching him. From this vantage, through the shack door, through a series of gaps in the old machinery, Charlie could see the drowned woman's feet.

"Have we met before? You look familiar to me. Are you from nearby?"

"No," Charlie said. "Idaho."

"You look familiar is all. You ever know a Charlene Elligsen?"

"No," Charlie said. "Not one I recall."

"There was a guy who used to run around with her sometimes. Used to see him coming and going. This would have been something like fifteen years ago."

Charlie shrugged.

"Huh. Well then you look a lot like someone I used to know."

Charlie had not thought about his appearance in a long time. Being called back into that visible existence, which he'd long ago either lost or discarded, inspired a vague uneasiness to well up in him. He felt his mind go to work closing those doors that had come ajar, and managing the floodgate of memory, and yet remote visions of his old life came to him as softly, and as indistinct, as voices conversing through the wall. Then the kid returned with the bucket brimming with water, sloshing some over the lip as he labored nearer, and Charlie remembered the fish that hung from the fishing line, wrapped tightly around his own dirty hand, which was just then purpling darkly from lack of circulation.

The kid set the bucket down at Charlie's feet. "There you go," he said.

Charlie lowered the trout into the water, which was murky with sediment from the lake floor. The fish slipped noiselessly to the bottom, where it lay still for a few moments, and then it turned itself upright and glided a lap around the bucket, which surprised Charlie. It had seemed dead in his hand. And yet there it was, claiming its last few moments of life, even with the line in its mouth and the hook in its gill.

"What do you know?" Charlie said. Then he looked at the kid. "Thanks for the fish," he said.

"Say 'you're welcome,'" the father told his son.

"You're welcome."

The boy's father smiled and scratched the stubble at his throat. "Listen," he said. "Figure we'll call it a day here. Going to head back to town soon." He looked at his son. "See what your mom's cooked up, huh?" He patted the boy's shoulder, then he peered up at the forest canopy and inhaled.

He waited for Charlie to reply, but Charlie only nodded and stared.

"All right," he said to his boy. "You ready?" Then the man turned his attention back to Charlie. "You know, if you were ever looking for a ride to town— It's gotta be a full day or so's hike, isn't it?" He glanced down at Charlie's bagged foot. "Well. We'd be happy to give you a lift, is what I mean. If you were looking to stock up on provisions or anything like that."

Charlie stood with his hands in his pockets and squinted down the dirt road, which disappeared into a gathering of pines.

"No," he said. "That's all right."

"Really, we have the room. Wouldn't be any trouble."

"There's a friend I'm out here with. He ought to be driving back in soon enough."

"Is that right?"

"Figure I'll wait for him."

"Right. Suppose it wouldn't be polite to leave him without saying so."

"I don't suppose so either."

"Right." The man seemed relieved. He exhaled. "Well. Saddle up, RJ." The kid tromped off to the car with an untied shoe. "Thanks for sharing your spot," the man said to Charlie.

"Well," Charlie said. "Not my spot anyway. Only where I'm set up."

"All the same," the man said.

"Thank you for the fish."

"Like I said, normally we catch and release."

Then they drove away and left Charlie with the forest's immense quiet and a fish in a bucket of lake water.

CHARLIE WENT BACK to the turbine house and stood above the drowned woman. He looked at her hair, which had dried in lank, clumpy strands. He felt, after the fishers' visit, he should check on her, though he wasn't sure why. It was not as if she could have left, and of course there was nothing she could need from him. Still, he stood above her and felt some sort of relief. So maybe she had meant to die, but he resolved that he would never understand what she had meant, and it felt as if he had given up a burden. "They seemed like good people," he said.

It troubled him dimly that he had been mistaken for another man. To have been mistaken for any living man at all was a surprise he had not thought to imagine, not in those days when his last and only company was a dead woman. He felt as though he himself had already suffered through some amount of dying. It had seemed to Charlie somehow impossible to ride into town with the father and son. He hadn't really considered the prospect at the time.

Charlie put another few pine boughs on the fire, though what reserve of firewood he had left was scant. The woodpile was reduced to a few twiggy limbs and a scatter of pine needles so that a stranger come upon it would not know it was a woodpile unless he'd been told so. The task of replenishing it, Charlie knew, was becoming too much for his foot. Though it was not just the foot anymore, he admitted to himself. The strength was leaving his arms, too. His hands were weights that he could not set down. It was troublesome to keep focused. A sort of smoke thickened in his mind. He was probably running a fever, it occurred to him, though when he placed the back of his hand on his forehead, his hand felt warm against his head, and his head felt warm against his hand. It was his skin, he decided. It was a whole warm suit of skin he wore, and it was a tottering scaffold of bones upon which he wore it.

Charlie took the fish from the water without any struggle. It floated there and watched Charlie's hand eclipse the sun, come down and pick it up, and then, without motion, the fish let the water pour off its body in a small shower. The smell of the fish and the water was pleasant, and the scales were slick and cool, and the fish's eye seemed as lifeless to Charlie as a marble, though the fish continued to open and close its mouth. He turned the fish belly-up in his grip and in a swing of the arm and swift snap of the wrist he cracked the fish's head against a stone. It was, undeniably, an easy way to go, Charlie thought—held in a great warm hand and killed instantly, with gratitude and without any malice.

There was no knife to clean the fish with, so Charlie used a nail, which he'd sterilized in the fire, to split the fish from end to end, moving slowly and messily, perforating a path he could tear apart with his fingers. The dark ribbon of innards, the red pebbled organs, the head and spine, Charlie collected into his palm and laid on the sun-warmed face of a broad stone. It would make for good bait if he could manage to walk to the creek. He put the fish on a stripped pine branch and leaned that over the fire and watched the skin roast and curl. For a while, he thought of nothing except the skin roasting and curling.

Say, for a second, Charlie thought, that he had taken that ride to town with the father and son. Where would he have gone once he arrived? Drop him off where? And then there was Sam. Charlie had said he would wait there to meet him. But really what it was, Charlie thought—the reason he hadn't seriously considered the offer— was his reeking foot. Imagine the smell of that awful foot trapped in the little cab of a pickup. Even with the windows down, imagine the boy pinching his nose and imagine the father shushing the boy's complaints and the boy not understanding why. No, it was not a thing a man could agree to on the spot. So that's that, Charlie told himself. Whatever future might have awaited him at the end of that ride to town was only a thing for imagining now and to imagine it any more could only weigh on his attitude. He knew Sam was not coming back. Sam was gone.

The fish was ready. He picked apart pieces of the white flesh and sucked his fingers and thought that he had eaten only crawdads for too long. Charlie thought he had never tasted anything so good as that trout. He only managed to eat half of it. His appetite was gone and he would save the rest.

Charlie was very tired and went to lie down. His pad and blanket were still laid beside the drowned woman in the corner of the turbine house. Though it was not raining, Charlie did not have the energy to move the pad back to the far, exposed corner and he decided he did not have the care to move it there either. So he settled down beside her again and looked up at the ceiling, where she too appeared to be looking. It was a pretty place. Easy to forget. After decades of disuse, the mortared stone walls and the rusted machinery were crowded with carvings of names and dates and obscenities and hearts. There was still sunlight in the window, but he knew the dark would meet him if he waited.

THE WEDDING PARTY

I'D MOVED INTO Ernie Prewitt's basement room for thirty-five dollars a week while my fiancée was packing up her things at our place. She had her sister in town to help. At the end of the month, when the lease ran out, she'd move inland, she told me. I hoped she'd change her mind before then, but I wasn't counting on it. She'd already given the ring back. Ernie was a mechanic at the marina where I worked. He had me set up with a cot nestled between his worktable and an array of props and grease-blackened engine parts. There was a transom-cracked skiff laid down and propped underside up against the far wall with a few dried-up barnacles still in a crowd on the hull and there was a single light overhead, a bulb and a chain, which rattled with the sound of Ernie's footsteps through the ceiling. The floor was unvarnished cement and cold and damp during the heavier rains. Sometimes Ernie's wife had leftover dinners, which she would leave for me in foil at the back door.

In the evenings I went to drink at this no-place seaside bar called Renny's Yard, where the wood-paneled walls were decorated with old harpoons and paddles and green glass fishing floats in sacks of netting. A picket of liquor bottles lined the mirror-backed bar, which seemed to double by its reflection. This night, as the sun went to a drab little ruby and slipped into the ocean, a wedding party showed up. I noticed them come in, all sunburnt and raw-eyed from the ocean water. The bride wore a new white sweatshirt, which said, in elaborate cursive, *Bride*. They bought their drinks and set up in the corner by the shuffleboard and the twin pool tables, and broke into a few groups, except for one young woman who trailed off aimlessly toward the bar. She wore a coral swimsuit cover-up, her bikini straps up and tied behind her neck, and her black hair pinned messily. Good God, I thought. The way she looked was something I felt in my guts. Her face was as small, and round, and as delicate, it seemed, as a bowl, which you might turn up in your hands and drink from. And before the shame of all my life could well up in me, as it usually did at such a pretty sight, she came over and said, "Want to buy a maid of honor something to drink?" Then we sat there for a while and got drunk on vodka sodas.

She told me her little sister was getting married tomorrow. She asked if I could believe that, and I said that I could. "She's beautiful, isn't she?" the maid of honor said. A couple of the guys she'd come with noticed her talking with me, and they seemed to discuss this a bit before losing interest and returning to their games. "Over there," she said. "See that guy—the one with the hair? The guy they're all crowded around? That's her fiancé." She took a drink and then shook the ice around in the glass to be sure it was finished. "He kissed me once," she said. "Back when him and Liz just started dating. Funny, huh?" She put her elbow on the bar and dropped her chin down onto her upward palm and looked at me as though I'd have something to say about that.

She looked like a TV lover with her skin glowing in the blue light from the neon beer sign mounted behind the bar. My fiancée had cystic fibrosis, which was why she was so small and which was why she'd had me, in the mornings, beat on her back with my open hands to knock the mucus loose from her lungs. What a vision of love, I thought: her hollow little body, her naked back, thumped like a drum in the paleness of the morning. And when, after she'd woken, she first spoke, her voice passed as softly through the room as the shadow of a bird. I guessed from the start that I would outlive her, even as she and I sat on the linoleum in the cold light of an open refrigerator door and drank champagne from mugs. The lonesomest thought of my whole life is that someday, like a stranger, I will hear it through the grapevine that she's died.

"What's your name?" I asked the maid of honor.

She looked at me with a devastatingly bored expression, and it sliced right through me. "Do you have any cigarettes?"

"Sure," I said.

"Let me have one." She hopped up from the stool and I followed her out to the patio, which was strung with strands of white Christmas lights. A Springsteen song was coming from a set of speakers by the hedges and an ashtray sat on a metal-mesh table, giving off the last few wisps of a dying cigarette that somebody had forgotten.

"I don't smoke," she said. "But I feel like one right now." I gave her a cigarette and lit it for her and lit one for myself. "Not that I care," she added, "if you think I smoke or not."

From there we could see her party through the window as they carried on without her. Her sister really was pretty. She looked to be one of the last sober members of the party, standing on the sidelines of a game of darts. The rest of them looked joyful and disarrayed, amused at the poorness of their aim at darts and pool. I sat on a bench by the door and the maid of honor dropped herself on my lap. She asked me what I did for a living, and then she said I'd need to make more money if I was ever going to marry her.

"We won't get married," I said.

"Guess how much my sister's ring cost," she said.

"I don't know."

"Guess."

I told her I didn't care how much it cost, which made her laugh, and then we kissed there for a while beneath a fluorescent wasp lantern hung from the awning.

The guy with the hair—the groom—came outside after a while and said, "Hey, Callie, Jen's looking for you." He held the door open with the heel of his shoe and waved her inside.

The maid of honor propped herself up with an elbow on my shoulder. "So tell her I'm out here."

"You can tell her yourself. Come on, Cal."

She spoke into my ear, but not in a whisper, so that I'm sure the beautiful groom could hear it all. "This is the one," she said. "This dreamy fella is the one marrying my dear little sissy. Didn't I tell you?" She said this into her hand cupped around my ear, and her breath was hot on my face. "Didn't I tell you that he kissed me?" She tossed her head back and laughed viciously. "And he'd have done more than that too if I'd have let him." And then she asked me, "Wouldn't you too? Wouldn't you do more if I let you?" She pressed her other hand lightly on my chest. "Oh, baby," she said. "That's what he kept saying—kissing my face all over. Oh, baby. Oh, baby. Like I was the prettiest girl in the world."

"Christ, Cal," the groom said. "You're shit-faced."

"Loosen up, handsome," she said.

The groom stared at us for a moment, and then he nodded at me. "Who's this guy?" he asked.

I began to say my name, but the maid of honor spoke up. "This is my new boyfriend. He's going to marry me just as soon as he gets a better job."

"I don't need this," he said.

And the maid of honor replied, "So run along, then." She kissed me with her eyes still on the groom. He sighed and went inside. I watched him through the window talking to the bride, gesturing at us, shrugging exasperatedly. The maid of honor took my chin in her fingers and directed my attention back to her, perched on my lap, and she kissed me again. Her chest, halfway dolloped on mine, gave me a vaguely homesick feeling.

"Would I be the prettiest girl you ever went to bed with?" she said.

I thought about this, and I lied. "It's hard to say," I said. "You'd be up there."

She took a drag from her cigarette and turned her attention out to the dark, out that way, where somewhere the ocean was heaving faintly.

"Where are you all staying?"

"What's that?" she asked. Before I could repeat myself, she groaned and said, "God, I'm so bored. If you marry me you can't be this boring."

I asked if she was always this way.

"Listen," she said, "my sister is the sweet one. You'd like her better than me."

"I think they're talking about you in there," I said, nodding to the window where the bride and groom had removed themselves to a corner of the room. The rest of the party went on while those two discussed something, it seemed, seriously, tiredly, and occasionally still gestured this way to the maid of honor and me.

She watched her sister for a while with her hand still set absently on my thigh as if it were not a thigh.

"Poor sissy," she said. "She's apologized for me her whole life." She was quiet for another moment. She said, "All the troubles of my life I made for myself. I know that. But even so, it never felt like I had much say in any of it. Are you listening?"

"Sure," I told her.

"It doesn't matter anyway. Listen," she said, "you should leave me alone for a minute. I can feel it. I'm just going to be mean to you. I can't help it. Come back in a minute and I'll be better to you, darling," she said. "You'll hardly recognize me."

So I left her alone for a minute. I slipped out from beneath her and settled her onto the bench, left her my pack of cigarettes and the lighter, and went off toward the bathroom. The wedding party grew quiet as I passed, and the boys leaned against their upright cue sticks with one arm over the other and the sticks heeled against the floorboards.

In the bathroom mirror I wasn't matching up quite right with my reflection. I sensed that the night was getting away from me. Then I heard a sort of commotion come muffled through the door. I went out to see. An argument had broken out between the maid of honor and her sister, and the groom was in the center, shouting along. The sister, for her part, never much raised her voice. She was crying though. I motioned toward them, but a couple of the groomsmen with their cue sticks shouldered into my path, and one held up a hand and said, "Hold off there, guy."

"It's all right," I said.

Another groomsman shouted over to me, "The night's ended. Why don't you get on, huh? Ask the bar for a taxi."

The groom had reached for the maid of honor's wrist, and she'd yanked it away and went on now even more loudly.

"All right," a bridesmaid shouted. "We're outta here. Close out. Load up!"

The members of the wedding party abandoned their games half-finished and settled their tabs while the groom and the bride and the maid of honor tussled out the door. I slipped out through the back exit down the hall by the bathroom and stumbled into the ocean night, where the lonely lamplight undid the small relief of the moon and the stars and threw everything past a certain distance into a deeper darkness.

I watched them argue for a while by a car with the door open. I couldn't hear the argument well, but now it had fallen to the maid and the groom, while the sister sat partway in the passenger seat of the car with her face in her hands. "Just get in the car, Cal," I heard the groom say.

And then she saw me half-shouldered into a yew shrub and she lit up with all her prettiness. She made for me, but the groom, from behind, wrapped his arms around her, pinning her arms against her sides, and began dragging her back toward the car. She kicked her legs up madly into the air and her pale skin shimmered faintly red in the car's parking lights.

"Darling," she shouted. "Darling, help!"

I had emerged into the lot now, it seemed. Already I was just a pace away from them, and already I was prying the groom's arms from

83

her waist. I'd only meant to set her loose, but in that wrestling mess of limbs I cracked the groom in the face with an elbow. Even if it's an accident, when you inflict an injury like this, especially against someone bigger than yourself, you can't leave it halfway done, and so, though I sure didn't want to, I cracked him again as good as I've ever cracked anyone. I surprised myself. You understand: He might have murdered me if I let him. He and the groomsmen might have savaged me with cue sticks and with billiard balls heavy as stones in their hands.

He buckled over and clutched his nose. "What the fuck?"

The bride was screaming. She rushed to the groom and tried to remove his hands from his face so that she could get a look at it.

The maid of honor took my hand and hurried me off. She stumbled to her knees once, and I lifted her up. "Come on," she said. "Your car. Where's your car?"

It was there, I told her, at the end of the lot, and she hopped around to the passenger side for a moment, yanking at the door, which I had to open from the inside, because everything I owned was half-broken. Emphatically, she told me to drive.

We tore off through the lot, clipping a curb as we went, and then a mailbox, which we pretty much demolished. The groom recovered himself and chased us into the street. The groomsmen and the bridesmaids followed after him and held out their empty hands and vanished as we turned a corner northbound onto Highway 101 with the coast beside us.

For a while she just laughed. I couldn't read her laughter at all. She said, "You hit him. I don't believe it. I bet he's never been slugged like that in all his life. Oh God," she said, and laughed again. "We're drunk. We're dumb drunk. You shouldn't be driving. It doesn't matter."

"I didn't mean to slug him like that," I said. My skin felt electric with adrenaline. I think I could have jumped ten feet straight into the air if I'd tried.

"It doesn't matter. Where's my bag?" she asked as she wrenched around. "Never mind. I don't have it."

It occurred to me then that my hand ached badly. There was a heartbeat in my knuckles. My three middle fingers went hot and stiff. I worked the shifter with my palm, thumb, and pinky and left my injured fingers alone to tremble and turn purple.

The highway was thin and empty and wove us along the coast in and out of the tree line. Dark ahead and dark behind. It was getting cold, but she opened the window anyway, and the cool, wet air tossed her hair around dimly in the cab.

"You rescued me," she said. "Now you probably expect things of me, yeah?"

"Or I stole you," I said. "Probably that's how it looked to them."

"Maybe it did. Maybe you've kidnapped me." She let out a shriek of laughter. "I've been kidnapped!" she shouted. "My fiancé's a lowlife kidnapper after all. Isn't it fitting? Where are you taking me, Killer Darling? What time is it?"

"I have a room that way," I said, pointing northwest into the shape of the hills rising against more distant hills, vaguely distinguishable as deepening shades of black.

"No," she said. "Not there. They'll find your name from the bar, and then your address, and then they'll find my blood all over your floor when they track you down. Even if you wash it away, it'll light up in those special lights they've got on the TV shows."

"Where, then?"

"Somewhere else. I shouldn't know where. It should be a secret."

"All right," I said.

"Oh God, his face. You caught him good. Sissy will need to put makeup on him for the ceremony. Imagine it. What are you doing?" she asked. "Don't get off here."

"I have a room that way."

"That's too depressing. God, I couldn't bear going to your room. Keep going. Good God. Keep going."

"Okay," I said, and turned off the blinker. And we went on, past a pillared rock formation out in the water and a few beach villages and the untenanted shopping center, and past a city fallen asleep without us.

"My grandparents lived down there," she said. She tapped the window. "Just there. Every summer when we were kids, we were down there. Grandma's living with Mom now, but that's where the house was."

The little seaside neighborhood was laid out in neat rows and lit periodically by lampposts so that I could make out, here from above, the skeleton grid of it, swerving around a bit on the road as I did.

She said, "That's why Sissy's wedding's here, right? I'd probably do it the same way if it were me. Not now. But I would've if I'd married first. No, I don't want you to get off here. Anywhere else."

She put her hand down on mine on the shifter and squeezed my crooked fingers. A lance of white agony carved, in an instant, up my arm and rattled my eyes like pill bottles.

"I wasn't getting off," I managed.

"You'll have to bury me. Knock me over the head first," she said. "Do you have a shovel, or will you dig my grave with your hands like a dog?"

I told her to cut it out. "It's not funny anymore," I said.

"Don't be so dull," she said. "Good God. Imagine me being murdered by a dull man. Good God! What are you even doing here? You don't live here, do you?"

"Yeah," I said. "I have a room back that way."

"I wonder sometimes—I used to wonder—passing through a Podunk spot like this, who the hell ends up living here?"

"I have a fiancée," I said. "That way."

"Do you?" She laughed. "When's the wedding?"

"She's moving to the city."

"So you don't have a fiancée, not except for me."

"Maybe that's right," I said.

"Don't mention her again," she said. "Please don't say anything else about that."

"All right."

"Do you have another cigarette?" she asked.

"I left them with you."

"No you didn't."

"Then no," I said, "I don't have any left."

We went on like this, not saying anything until it seemed like time to turn back and she told me to pull off at the approaching exit. "Here," she said. "This is a good spot." And so we traced up this little peninsula, low against the ocean.

She asked me the name of where we were, but I didn't know. I hadn't seen the sign. The road was old and frayed to hunks at the edges, and the spikerush lit up in the headlights. A roadside ditch of brackish water. A few old houses. A few short fences. Gravel parkways. Unlit windows. No, I had no idea where we were. We parked where the road turned to dirt at the foot of some larger building, which extended on stilts into the water, and we saw, revealed in the headlights on a weatherworn sign, that it was a cannery. The maid of honor tumbled from the car, leaving the door open, leaving the interior light pooling on the uneven lot. She leapt out into the dark and I went after her.

There were great, pale mounds silhouetted against the nighttime, heaped as tall as trucks around the lot. I studied them for a moment from a distance, and her weaving happily between them, but I didn't know what they were. "Come here," she said, returning to me. She took my outstretched hand, my good one, and pulled me against her as she kissed me, then she collapsed with me down onto a mound, which crunched beneath our weight and jutted into my back and shed a clicking skate of oyster shells over us.

"Shucked shells," I said, taking one in my hand and tossing it. "It's all oyster shells." The smell was like the gut of the ocean, sweet and salty and ruined. No more meat or pearl. Just the boneyard beneath us.

She took a shell in her hand and stood up and studied it, pushing her thumb across its nacre belly. She thought about this a moment and then looked around. I watched her for a while. From the corner of my eye, the shadow shapes of the place—the oyster middens, an outhouse down the way, rusted trailers and rusted barrels—trembled by the beating of my heart and seemed alive. And her, was she cold, I wondered? Were the hairs on her arms standing up? What wordless thoughts were pulsing in her dumb-drunk head as she peered from that dimness into the dark?

"I think I've been here before," she said. She took a few steps one way, paused, and then took a few steps the other way. It was a birdless night. Only the sound of the combers offshore, rolling the sea over in the black and far away. She still had the shell in her hands. "Why'd you bring me here?"

"You told me to," I said.

"I think I've been here before."

"Where are we?"

"That way," she said. "Out that way there's an old schoolhouse with red shutters. If it were light out, it'd be right that way and you'd see it. And there was a pier. Did we pass it? I've been here before. We ate oysters at a table on a cannery deck."

She walked on slowly through the low grass, which was dipped with moonlit puddles. We navigated the shallow slope with our feet and hands, palming our way along the unpainted clapboard of the cannery house until the earth turned to rocks and submerged into the comings and goings of the tide.

"When I was a kid," she said, "there was a boy I used to run around with. He took me here. His daddy had died just before, and he drove me around in his daddy's old truck all up and down the coast. I haven't thought about him in years, until just now, and all of a sudden I sort of miss him again."

I stood a few paces to her back and watched as she wrapped her arms around herself and braced against the ocean breeze, which whistled in the grass.

"Has that ever happened to you?" she asked.

"Which part?"

"Something like that."

"Maybe so," I said. "I can't remember."

"I'm sorry," she said.

"What for?"

"Oh, I don't know anymore. Forget it. Sometimes I have this feeling like I've never once said what I really meant to say. I'm ready to see the place where you live now." Then she dropped the shell at her feet and went off to the car.

WRECK

I WENT A DAY ahead of my brother-in-law, out to Burns, to get a lay of the bike trails. This brother-in-law of mine—Rod's his name—was new to the sport. I didn't want to push him too hard or else we'd be walking our bikes out of there in the dark in our pedal clips. I rode the first leg of a blue square I figured Rod could handle, and a black diamond I wanted a chance at on my own, then I drove out through the forest corridor and the sagebrush desert, took an early dinner at—I'm sorry to say—an awful brew pub on the Silvies River, then went for an evening walk out at the falls, a ten, twenty-minute drive outside of town. I was thinking in an abstract way about suicide. My sister, Andi, had been worried about my state of mind. The week before, I'd neglected to return her phone call and she nearly sent the police out for a wellness check. I don't know exactly what I'd said to make her panic. Suicide honestly hadn't occurred to me.

Five months earlier, my wife went to a poet's wedding in Florida and never came back. She told me over the phone that she'd had an epiphany, like a bolt of lightning, presumably right after she'd slept with the cellist, that she hadn't been in love with me for years, maybe never at all. She really couldn't remember. I gave Andi every gruesome detail, which I wouldn't have done had I still been in possession of my head. I wondered if it sometimes happens that way—suicide, that is. Maybe the decision arrives to some as a vague, half-hearted notion without your full awareness, such as, for instance, a man driving a straight road at high speed, daring himself to close his eyes for however many seconds at a time, or, I imagined, say, a woman, after two glasses of wine, using the balustrade of her hotel balcony as a balance beam. And look at me, I thought, standing on a narrow dirt path myself, with the river rolling at a man-killing distance below. What was I really up to anyway? Nothing risky, I swear.

It's a very high country out there, cracked in half by a narrow but deep river gorge. Over one way are the falls, which I'd seen torrential in the spring with snowmelt, but now, late fall, it ran just a trickle. Down the other way a trail climbs over a rocky promontory, then descends half a mile at most in switchbacks along the escarpment, passing the decommissioned dam on its way, half-buried in the adjacent slope, landing finally on a sandy shore at a meander in the river, a pool of clear, green water. My wife and I had a romantic moment once on that river beach, years ago, which I'm sure must be the reason I returned. I don't know what I expected. The sun was halving itself over the western rimrock. A chill rode on the wind. It was all-around lonesome and very beautiful.

I stopped watching where my feet were going for a moment, looked up, and there she was. On an outcropping of stone pressed out over the gorge, I saw a fluttering red dress, wearing a mess of wind-thrown hair. The dress was sleeveless and so the woman was bare-shouldered in the cold. What business, I wondered, did anyone have wearing that dress in this terrain and weather, or at this hour, and without company? For a few moments I watched the woman in the distance, feeling spooky about the night, thinking, how weird, as she stood above the ravine in the coursing wind. It struck me then that maybe I was about to watch this woman die.

I'd entertained thoughts of suicide too head-on, too frivolously, and in that way I'd put a dare to God or whomever—such were the toddler-like workings of my subconscious brain. Now I'd summoned a suicidal woman to teach me a lesson. I hurried down the uneven trail in the low light, chancing the switchbacks at a jog, losing sight as I did of the woman on the ledge in the air. And what would I even say to her? Please, miss, don't? Let's reconsider? And another thought I had: I'm going to eat it going like this, rock dodging on the precipitous decline, and then I did. Twenty or so yards out, my foot caught an exposed root or rock or such, and I went ass up and over. Down on the ground I found a low stone shelf with my elbow. Adrenaline, though, pinched me up by the nape, landed me on my feet, carried me to the ledge where I'd glimpsed the woman. It required a bit of scaling to reach. I managed. It wasn't pretty.

I worried I'd find the ledge already empty by the time I'd hoisted myself up, but instead I found, as it turned out, two of her. I didn't know what I was looking at. There was the one woman I'd seen in the red dress—she was fine, had not jumped, gave no indication of jumping now—and somehow, at the woman's side, my God, I thought, there she was again, in a puffy coat, holding an expensive-looking camera. She'd multiplied herself. Same woman, two of them, both pink-nosed in the cold. Wide eyes, dimpled cheeks, the heart faces—all the same. I would understand later of course that the women were twins, but for just these few moments, in my mystification, I'd forgotten what twins were and was astounded to find two identical women in the middle of nowhere. I loitered in the narrow stone passage, panting. My head was on roller skates, my pant leg, I saw then, torn open, scraped-up kneecap crowning into the cold canyon wind. The identical sisters watched me uneasily, cornered against the high cliffside plunge. We were in the middle of nowhere, I remembered. I could have murdered them both without consequence. I became aware of myself again, the bloodied, wild-eyed man I resembled.

"It's slick," I said, hearing my own dumb voice with discouragement. "It's a long way down."

"We're being careful," the photographer twin said. She had her finger on the shutter button of her camera as if she were debating whether or not to take my picture.

I looked down at myself, feeling pitiful. "I guess I'm not."

The woman in the dress touched her forehead and told me I was bleeding there, which, as it turned out, I was, though not too badly. Suddenly it began to pulse itself into a demanding nuisance, my temple throbbing first, then all over—my back, my arm, the knee. It was as if her words had ignited the pain. How could you, I thought, when I only wanted to save your life?

LATER THAT NIGHT Rod arrived at the motel, took a look at my face, and said, "What's this, Pat! Are we jousting with trees?" Rod's an esteemed physician. He inspected my head wound and told me what I'd been hearing a lot lately: I'd live. Rod's a good guy. He's loaded, very fit, devoted to his two boys and to Andi, and makes marriage look easy and dignified. Rod's got it all going for him. Now and then I felt like holding it against him, but he's very likable. He's a bigwig at the hospital. You'd never know it. He never talks about work. I saw him on the local news once, providing the expert opinion on a salmonella outbreak in the alfalfa harvest. I said, Rod, I saw you on the TV! And Rod said, Can you believe that? After my separation, he and Andi found every excuse to check in on me. They live sixty miles up the Columbia River and still they wound up at my door three, four times a month. Andi, nine years my elder, had never been more my sister than she was in those days of my heartbreak. Our parents, who were years dead by then, would be glad to know. Sometimes Rod came by on his own as an emissary of my sister's concern, and on such occasions Rod and I took out the road bikes and spoke as though Andi were listening from the bushes. Now and then my divorce came up, but what's there to say? It's tough. It feels awful. A lot of people have done it before me. Life gets better for some and smaller for others. When conversation left us, we just pedaled harder until we thought of something else.

Earlier I wrote that my wife went to a Floridian's wedding and never came back, which is true in spirit, but of course she did come back. She had to. I still had all her stuff in the garage. We had the house to sell. We had bank accounts to separate. And because vanishing instantaneously wasn't an option, she tried to approximate the effect by rushing through the proceedings as quickly as possible. Eight nights in a motel and then she was off to her mother's in North Carolina. I've seen years in my life less eventful than the one month of our divorce. It was like waking up in the hospital after an accident and finding things much as they were except, toss the bedsheet aside, and you seem to be missing a leg now.

The affair, she'd said, was a one-off, drunken episode, but it clarified things for her. Why'd she tell me at all? So that I'd stop asking her to slow down and reconsider. She arrived with her heart in armor, wearing a grim, unsympathetic face. We closed on the house three weeks prior to my trip to Burns. In the meantime, I had a short-term lease in the armpit of northeast Portland. Catalytic converters were at a premium and vanished often. The neighbor lady next door spent the mornings insulting her little dog in the yard as it dallied to complete its business. The couple upstairs had a shouting match every night and existed only between the hours of one and four a.m. At her first visit, I thought Andi was about to tear up. She kept it together. She said, "You could walk to the grocery store from here."

Rod and I shared a motel room in Burns at the Rory & Ryan Inn, which he sprang for. I think Rod may actually have been close to a millionaire at that time. He could have rented two rooms for the year and not even felt it. Over the course of the evening, I thanked him a dozen times. He sat against the headboard of his bed and me at mine. We had a couple beers on the nightstand with a true crime show on the TV, in which a young actress reenacted the acid torture of a real-life prostitute. The encounter with the twins had left me in such a funny mood that I failed to notice Rod was also in a funny mood until he apologized. I didn't know what he was talking about. I'd been wondering what the liquid was that they threw on the young actress. "I'm not giving you much conversation to work with," Rod said. "I have my head up my ass tonight, Pat. I'm too tired to go retrieve it."

I'd expected the stiltedness was my fault, as had been the case lately, but then, turning to Rod on the bed, I saw he was staring straight through the wall. Still had his shoes on. Andi and he put Monty down that very morning, he said—their spaniel, a king cavalier. A couple days earlier Andi had the electric fondue pot heating up on the kitchen island; she had a shrink-wrapped tray on the countertop of thumb-sized bits of meat and vegetable. Monty, smelling the meat, running around, going nuts—as was his way—got himself tangled in the power cord. Pulled the pot of oil down onto his back. Andi and Rod were out on the patio with a bottle of wine when they heard it, the boys up in their rooms playing video games. If a dog gets second- and third-degree burns all over its body, the veterinarian does not do skin grafts. Poor Monty had all his hair coming off. He was only three years old. They slathered him in Vaseline, wrapped him in a wet towel, and took him to the vet, where he was kept under observation for two nights. Eventually they had to face facts. "We just had to look at Monty," Rod said, "and ask, what are we putting you through?"

I told Rod that was a horrific story. "And, Christ!" I said. "That was this morning, as in the morning of today?" Except, what about Andi, I wanted to know. We'd spoken on the phone last night and the night before both, and there wasn't a word about Monty. There wasn't even a hint in her voice. "Why didn't Andi say so on the phone?" I asked. "We were on for an hour at least."

Rod thought about this. He was always very careful when speaking on Andi's behalf. "Ah," he said. "Well, she knew we had our trip coming up. I guess she didn't want to bum anyone out."

"I wish she'd just told me," I said.

"I'm sure she'll get around to it," Rod said. "You know how she is. She won't tell you like it's any breaking news. She'll go, oh, by the way, speaking of fondue."

Then Rod asked if he should be nervous. He nodded to the beer in my hand, which I was holding like an ice pack against my abraded forehead. If the trail had knocked me off my seat, he said, he had to wonder how he'd fare out there. So I told him, actually, it hadn't happened on the trail. Long story, Rod; ends with me on my ass, and so on. I wasn't sure what to say about the women I'd frightened. I was still deciding what they meant to me. Rod raised an eyebrow.

"I was trying to save a woman's life," I said.

Rod nodded thoughtfully. "Did you succeed?"

"No," I said. "I just messed up my face."

He said, "Well, we can't save them all."

IN THE MORNING Rod showed me his new bike. He picked it up the week before. I'll say it again: Rod's loaded. It was an extravagantly nice mountain bike for a man who'd never ridden one. Whoever had Rod at the bike shop sold him on every up-charge. He had me take it around the motel lot. Over the years I'd gotten my own bike, part by part, just the way I wanted it, but Rod's was a spectacle just to look at. Also decorating Rod's garage: a windsurfing board, two stand-up jet skis from the eighties, three road bikes (two of them Cannondales and one an incredible Cervélo), an elaborate home brew setup, golf clubs, a Remington over-under, a fly rod, two pairs of snow skis. I told him, now that's one nice bike, Rod.

"I figured, hey, if I like it out there, I won't have to upgrade down the line."

"You can't blame it on the equipment if you don't," I said. Then I turned another lap around the lot before we loaded the bikes up into his giant Ford and went out into the wilderness.

Rod and I rode all afternoon. Mountain biking, it's a terrific postdivorce activity. You don't have the bandwidth to think about anything except the turn in the trail. You're making quick decisions or else you're going over your handlebars. Wife, what wife? What's a cellist? Sometimes you go airborne. There's thrill involved. I've never made great money, don't know anything about engines, and I enjoyed having one rugged hobby to feel tough about. Rod was keeping up. I'd stopped looking over my shoulder for him. He had thighs like he could kick your head off. We reached our halfway mark, wiped our faces, had lunch, turned back for the truck, another seven miles to go, and then Rod hit a rock in the worst way available. Rod got tossed.

I hardly heard it happen. I'd been in front, leading the way. When I looked back, the trail was empty.

I found Rod at the foot of a low rocky climb on his back and up-side down on the trail slant so that his legs were up slightly above his head. Was he hurt, I asked, although I could see he was hurt. In fact, he was hurt badly. No blood had appeared, but he was clutching his body as if to keep his organs from swapping places. Rod made a terrible noise when he inhaled. He looked at me upside down.

"I think I broke my back," he said.

Now, I didn't know what happens when a back is broken. I asked more than once if he could feel his toes. I thought to myself, if Rod's in a wheelchair after this—if this is the news I have to give my sister on the phone, that after an attempt at brightening my spirits, your husband will require a wheelchair for the rest of his life—I really would kill myself, not half-heartedly. I would write the letter and make for certain.

"I'm worried about my lungs," Rod said.

I stood above Rod and waited for him to tell me what to do, but he had all his attention on getting air in and out of him. If it had been me on the ground, at least I would have had a doctor on hand.

"I need to get right side up," he said. "Let's get my legs pointed that way."

"Hold on, Rod. Don't they say—I don't think I'm supposed to move you, Rod."

"Right now, you're supposed to," he said. "Point me that way."

I hunched over him in an awkward way, took his thighs up, and dragged him around so that all the blood wasn't rushing to his head anymore. His whole face clenched up as we went, but I saw his feet moving on their own. He hissed spit out of his mouth in frothy spurts. There wasn't any cell reception out there and we were seven miles from the truck. It was not a quick, easy seven miles—hairpin turns, sudden climbs, inopportune boulders. The sun was going low in the sky. I held my phone over my head and cursed. Rod wasn't going anywhere or saying anything. He lay battered on the trail as if he'd just dropped from the treetops overhead.

I realized now I should have started Rod off on something a bit easier, but I hadn't wanted to infantilize him, and I hadn't wanted him to think he'd mastered anything else on his first try. The trail's midway point we'd just left—a little clearing of gravel with an ancient picnic table and an outhouse—sat aside a service road, which cut back to the highway. I'd seen as much on the map the day before. I still thought a better plan would occur to us. How could I leave Rod as he was? His every breath required such an effort I worried I'd have to get down and start blowing into his mouth at any moment. If nobody were watching Rod, I thought he might evaporate. He considered his situation for a long time, exploring the sharp contours of his pain, saying nothing, and then, finally he said, "Okay. Go find reception." The EMTs would come with a stretcher, he said. No clearing big enough for a life flight. "When you get them on the phone," Rod said, "tell them, pneumothorax. Say, spinal trauma."

I really can't stress enough how terrible his voice was, the ragged, chunking breaths he drew, the wheezing, wordless utterances of agony. He had dirt on his lips, tilting into his mouth, and paid it no attention.

I said, "I really hate to leave you out here." Then I gave Rod my water and mounted my bike and turned to leave. Rod called to me with the little bit of voice he had left in his lungs. "Not your fault, bud. Don't think it. It'll just slow you down."

I wasn't sure if Rod was wrong or lying. Because I knew whose fault it was, and it did not slow me down. I was the fastest man alive.

I RIPPED BACK up the trail, took the service road, and forty-five minutes later I was busting ass on the empty highway. I'd left my windbreaker behind, tied around the trunk of a young pine to mark the entrance to the service road. I had my phone out, looking for reception bars to appear. Burns sits at the edge of what's sometimes called Oregon's empty quarter, the untenanted southeast quadrant of the state, a vast, aboriginal nothingness for the next two hundred miles or more. I was starting to think I'd made the wrong decision. I should have taken the trail maybe, taken the truck back to town at a hundred miles an hour. In fact, I couldn't remember deciding on my present course of action at all, or by what logic I'd arrived at the plan. An hour ago I was a totally different person. Maybe I wouldn't get cell service until I got all the way to Burns, and Burns, by bike, was at least a three, four-hour ride. Rod was in the dark now, maybe aspirating for all I knew, wondering if he'd been forgotten. I was trying to do math at high speed. If I turned back, I could make it to the trailhead and the truck in—I wasn't sure—maybe an hour by the highway, but I'd still have to make the drive. However I looked at it, I thought I was screwed. I pedaled on with the unbearable feeling that I was pedaling in the wrong direction.

It's awful that it required a disaster first, but I decided now that Rod obviously belonged to the highest order of men who'd ever lived. Not elitist, just elite, supreme. Generous and humble, kind and rich, with a tremendous capacity for grace and a remarkable body for a man of his late forties. I remembered a dinner party years ago at Andi and Rod's. My wife and I were both there, and a partner of Rod's from the clinic came with his wife, along with another couple that left zero impression on me whatsoever. We'd just finished an incredible meal. Andi was pouring wine like a frat boy. She had a little parrot in those pre-children days, which sat on his perch at the window, calling out, "Cookie, cookie." We lazed about reclined and overfull on the couches and traded our heartfelt experiences so far of aging—debts coming due on years of bad posture, a now-familiar susceptibility to world-ending hangovers, the gentle, steady goodness of a heart that wasn't on fire all the time. I asked Rod if he remembered how, as a young man, he could press up from an L-sit on the floor straight into a handstand. My uncle goaded him into it once when he was in his early twenties, at a family function. I was just a boy and it had amazed me then. Rod thought about my question for a moment, then, saying nothing, set his wineglass down on the windowsill, sat in an L on the carpet, and he lifted himself, threaded his legs and his pointed toes right through his arms, and levered his torso up over his head into a perfect handstand. For just a moment the room was silent in wonder of Rod with his toes to the ceiling. The window behind him was brilliant with daylight. It was his partner, I think, who broke the spell by hooting, and then we fell into applause and the bird in the corner called out, "Cookie, cookie." I said, "My God, someone should be filming us." I had my wife under my arm. Whatever she says about it now, we were in love back then. I remember it on her face. Actually, what I really remember now is when, on our way out the door, we thanked Andi for the incredible meal.

"I only picked out the wine," she said. "The rest was all Rod."

AFTER ANOTHER HOUR pedaling in the dark, I heard an engine far off at my rear. A pair of headlights summited the rise in the road and winked into view like distant match strikes. I dropped my bike on the asphalt and waved my arms madly. I was prepared to be run over if that's what it took. I'd take a ride to town as a spatter of blood on the windshield. When the car at last put its blinker on, there were tears in my eyes. The sedan came to rest a few paces ahead at the gravel shoulder and waited there for me. I stood my bike against a tree.

I saw through her open window that my rescuer was a beautiful young woman in hiking wear. There'd been an accident, I told her, and what I needed more than anything was a ride into town. I thanked her for stopping and she invited me in. She had a passenger, a second woman with a beautiful back of the head, and beside me in the back seat were a few beautiful pieces of obsidian as big as your fist. I asked if they had reception on their cell phones. The passenger lit the cab up with her screen, then turned to me to say, "I'm not getting anything here," but I hardly heard her. I could see her clearly now. The woman in the passenger seat wore the face of the woman in the driver's seat. For the second time in two days, I nearly forgot what twins were.

I had to apologize for laughing. "I'm just surprised," I said. "I'm just so grateful."

"But," the passenger said, with care in her voice, "you're not laughing." And I saw she was right. I was crying again. "Of course!" I said. Then I put my face in my hands.

I told the god-sent twins about Rod, the wreck, the fool's rescue mission I was on, even my divorce came up in a passing way as the occasion for everything. It all poured out of me like heartbreak soup at their footwells. But we were already back on the road. I saw we were moving. The twin in the passenger seat had her cell phone above her head, out the window, looking for service, face in the wind. The twin driving had the pedal to the floor, which, I thought, was the most wonderful thing I'd ever seen. The dotted line rushed by us like machine-gun fire. One sister turned to the other and said something that wasn't meant for me. "Now you know," she said. "This is what it feels like to go a hundred miles an hour."

I'd wondered earlier that morning if I might encounter the twins in town, as small as it was, at one of the five restaurants, say, or the two grocery stores, maybe next door at the motel. I wasn't sure I'd survive the embarrassment. The worry had me walking around with my head down, averting my eyes. Then I go stepping into their car anyway. I wished my father were alive—not in the general way that I miss him a little every day, but in the way that'll make you halt in your steps halfway up the stairs. He believed in fateful coincidences. He'd have liked this part. Only if he knew Rod turned out okay.

I asked the twins if they could believe the odds. How's that? one asked. Well, that it would be them, of all people, to find me, I said. "After our meet-cute disaster at the falls last night," I said. "I'm not making this up, am I?"

The twin riding passenger turned around in her seat to see me better. Her sister found me in the rearview mirror. "No way," she said. "It's the guy."

"Who?" her sister asked from the driver's seat. She studied me in the mirror. "Oh."

For a split second I worried they'd ask me, on second thought, to please step out of their car. But I got lucky. I saw that they were wonderful, kind women with charitable hearts and a gentle sense of humor. They thought it was all some kind of cosmic joke, and I agreed. I apologized again. "I got back to my motel last night," I said, "saw myself in the mirror, you know, my busted face, and I thought, those poor women!"

"Anyone can fall on their face," the driver said.

"It's just that I saw you up on that ledge," I said, "in your dress, and, I don't know! I mistook myself for a goddamned hero or something."

Except I didn't know which had been the twin in the dress, and which the photographer. There was no dress or camera to tell them apart this time. They were each dressed as weekend hikers in flannel shirts and new shell jackets. They even wore their hair the same, piled neatly on top of their heads. When I spoke to the twins, they were both the woman in the dress.

The twin in the passenger seat leaned over the console and shook my knee. "Isn't that just how it goes?" she said.

When we finally found reception, I could already see the little city of Burns gathered dimly on the horizon. The twins drove me on to the Rory & Ryan Inn, as I detailed, to the best of my ability, the exact whereabouts of Rod to the operator on the emergency line: the name of the trail—incidentally, it was called Baby Skull, for who knows what grim reason—the service road, the nearest milepost, my windbreaker marking the way. Take the western arm of the trail, I said, to the left, about a mile and a quarter, and my brother-in-law will be the man on the ground. Was she really getting this all down? Miss any of this information, and they'd miss Rod, too. The further I went in my directions, the clearer Rod appeared to me dead on his gurney.

I removed myself from the twins' car and saw I'd left a perfect impression of my ass in sweat on the nylon upholstery. I was still on the phone, but I wanted to thank the sisters on my knees. They saw it on my face. The twin in the passenger seat pressed her fingers to her mouth before she waved me away, as if to say, No need. Then they drove off as namelessly as they'd twice arrived.

My next call was to Andi. She knew something was wrong before she heard my voice. She was on the road before we hung up. Me too. I jumped into my car and hightailed it back to the woods to be sure Rod was found. I still had Andi terse and weepy in my ear when a beautiful sight presented itself to me: I turned onto the service road and an ambulance squeezed past me going the opposite way, flashing its otherworldly lights in the pitch-dark forest.

"They're really cooking," I told her. "Andi, they're cooking like a damn rocket ship."

"Thank you, God," she said. "Follow them to the hospital, Pat. Call me when you've seen him. Get off the phone. I'm hanging up on you, Pat." And she did.

IT TOOK THE emergency crew three hours to find Rod, check him out, load him into the ambulance, and deliver him to the hospital. Andi got to the hospital by two in the morning, not long after they rolled Rod in on his gurney, heaped in misery. When she stepped through the sliding doors and got a look at me, Andi right away feared the worst. She said, "Tell me." All I could do was gulp on my breath. I nearly gave her a heart attack. The nurse had to step in and sort us out. Rod was okay, the nurse said. He cracked a vertebra and four ribs, and all we could do about that was take it slow and easy and let him grit his teeth. In other words, he hadn't collapsed a lung, but he did break his back.

"He's very lucky," the nurse said. "The trails up there make three or four paraplegics a year. Your husband, by the grace of God, is not one of them. I'm gonna remind you of that again after you've seen him." Then she took us to Rod. Even on the pain meds, he was reduced to just pain and discomfort. He was pissed off at himself and exhausted. He'd already asked the doctors everything worth asking. As sorry a shape as he was in, Rod was still the finest doctor to ever pass through the halls of Harney District Hospital. The doctors gave Andi papers to fill out. When she finished, she put the cap on the pen and turned and told me, "You're still wearing your bike shorts."

Andi and I took a couple hours' rest in the motel. It was light when we woke. We checked back in at the hospital and then she gave me a ride out to Baby Skull to retrieve Rod's truck and our bikes. She hadn't packed a bag. She was wearing Rod's flannel shirt and sunglasses. "Hey, Rod," she said, in her best impression of me as a meathead, "let's start you out nice and easy, huh? I know the perfect place: *Baby Skull.*"

She dropped me at the trailhead with Rod's truck and his keys, then pulled her car around and pointed herself to the highway. She rolled down her window. "Pat," she said, and waved me to her. She said, "Come here, little brother," but she already had ahold of my sleeve. She pulled my top half in through her driver-side window and squeezed me around my shoulders.

When I returned to the hospital, Rod wasn't in his bed. Andi stood at the window. "He's getting some air," she said. "Did you find your bikes?"

I had. Mine stood at the same tree along the highway, and Rod's lay where it had fallen on the trail. I rode it back up to the service road where I'd parked Rod's pickup and I thought to myself, No, Rod definitely could not blame the equipment. It was a marvelous bike with a beautiful geometry, light and precise and stable at speed. I was grateful to find it and I never wanted to see Rod on it again. I told Andi I had both bikes back at the motel.

"That's good," she said. "Crisis averted."

I joined her at the window and saw Rod was down there in a wheelchair. The hospital didn't want him standing up just yet without a spotter, although Andi told me he'd managed a handful of excruciating steps from the bed to his wheelchair. Rod had his gown on, sitting at the foot of the lawn. It was a beautiful day, a low blue sky and a high float of clouds sailing into view. Andi and I watched Rod until she was satisfied it was nothing to worry about, then she sat in an armchair with her head tilted back and closed her eyes for a while. We'd come such a distance from our own lives, shipwrecked in this hospital suite, and yet the world seemed to be right where we left it, right there out the window. What did I expect? The buildings were upright. Trees stood in the dirt. A little dog led an old man down the sidewalk. A pickup arrived at the stop sign with a woman in its open passenger window. Rod waved to her. She dropped her cigarette on the road and then zoomed away, carrying her whole, enormous life in her head.

EMERGENCY MANEUVERS

W E THREE BROTHERS spent the afternoon outside in the volcanic haze and half rain. We trekked the empty field out behind the decommissioned paper mill where our father used to work and we were fallen upon by ashes from Mount St. Helens, which had erupted three days earlier, and once more two days after. The wind took most of the ashes east, as far, they said, as Oklahoma, but there was still the gray silt here in Oregon, and the car tread through it on the roadways like through a snow dusting. Spring drizzling turned the ash to a fine black mud, which stole the smell of the earth from the air, as if the grass and the trees and overgrowth would stop growing for good. I imagined that we would live out our lives in these gray ruins, and we would describe someday to children of our own how the world had looked when there was still green in the hills and red poppy blossoms on the shoulder of the highway and blackberry bramble winding down to the runoff pond near the overpass where we had once watched nutria loitering in the mud and the cattails.

Carson, who was fifteen and the oldest of us, found a wooden boomerang beneath an ashy clump of grass, which he tore free and tucked into the back of his jeans as if it were a pistol. He had a knack for finding things. He hiked on, up over the low rocks, and beneath us the country rolled downfield to a gray wasted farmland and a gray distance farther on, into which everything seemed to vanish.

"Throw it, then," said Levi, who was ten—the youngest of us. He always wore shorts and spent much of our outings plucking grass burrs from his skin and tending to thorn pricks on his shins.

Carson shook his head. Levi asked him why not.

"If it doesn't come back, I won't find it again." He waved his arm at the impenetrable thickets of blackberry vines.

I said if it didn't come back, then it was broken anyway. Carson said it wasn't broken and untucked his shirt from behind the boomerang so that we could only see the outline of it beneath the fabric. Carson had a colorful bruise on his cheek, which he'd returned with one afternoon after school and said nothing about.

Our house was small, but we had enough property to house two cars that Dad had long planned to get running again, and an old 125cc dirt bike, which was rusted out, and then behind the shed, beneath a black tarpaulin, Dad's Ford Ranger, which was in danger of repossession. Our mother's recent absence robbed the home of its warmth. Maybe some of that, too, was the bit of ash hanging in the air, dimming the light in the windows.

For the last week, our mother had been an hour's drive south in Coburg with our grandmother and our aunt and with our grandfather who was dying. Grandpa never liked Dad and Dad never liked him, and neither went to any lengths to hide their feelings. If ever our grandparents came to visit, Dad hid beneath the truck with a wrench or went fishing until they'd left. What frightened me most was not the idea of our grandfather dying. I hardly knew him. It was the thought that his death might change our mother so that she would become less like our mother.

She said Grandpa saw skyscrapers where there were not skyscrapers. Last time she picked him up for lunch, she told us he leaned his head against the passenger window as they drove, looking up at the sky, and he'd said, "I know they're not really there."

"Maybe he's just seeing the future," Dad said later.

"There's no future," she said, "no matter how distant, that sees Coburg, Oregon, as a bustling metropolis."

"Who knows?"

"Coburg will get smaller every day until its small enough to blow away in the wind. He's dying. I don't expect you to care."

"All right."

"I wish you'd care for my sake at least."

"Sure," he said. "I wish that too." He finished his drink and our mother went to bed and we three brothers listened through our door, cracked only enough to let in the muffled ghosts of their voices and a slip of light, which bent along the wall and caught Levi's pupil so that it lit up like a cat's.

The paper mill was in the process of being torn down and the jagged metal innards of it, exposed, reminded me of a very large ship with the hull broken off. Our father had worked on the floor on machine number two. When they'd shut the plant down, first they shipped off what machinery they could sell. Great rows of trucks carted it all away. You could see them going from our front window. Dad said to us—as he traced the procession's path down the highway—"I've turned every screw on that machine twice." He was more familiar with the press and rollers than he was with our mother. It was only once that I crept into the kitchen in the morning and saw my father behind my mother, with his arms around her waist and his chin on her shoulder. It was only the once, so I've kept this memory close. Dad used to come home with grease-black hands and go immediately to the sofa, where he'd sit, for a moment, with his boots still on.

Now, with the mill gone, Dad haunted his own home, and didn't know what to say to us who lived there. He woke early in the blue-black mornings, and in the afternoons we watched him pass in and out of the room and then in again, as though there'd been something he'd meant to do, except he couldn't remember what it was.

My brothers and I stood there in the ash fall and listened to the distant sound of the last few tinkerers in the mill, stripping the copper piping and wires and throwing it all in flatbeds. These were its last days, and the sun was already setting, and we were there on the other side of the fence.

That morning I'd sat outside alone to watch the sun come up through the trees, as I often did, and I saw, across the yard, between two unkempt blueberry bushes, a deer standing like the statue of a deer, which ran off after a moment that felt much longer than it was. There was ash in the deer's fur. The image occurred to me throughout the day, and sometimes even still. There seemed to be very little to say about it, so I never mentioned it to my brothers—the deer and the ash and how it seemed to come to life.

Levi was the first to catch the sound of a motor approaching. Our father's pickup climbed the hill and tossed up a small rooster tail of ash.

"He's coming," Carson said.

"What for?" Levi said.

Carson shrugged. "Us, I guess."

I said maybe the repo man was snooping around again. Dad had been parking his pickup on the edge of Shelby's lot next door, beneath a gathering of plum trees, which Shelby had neglected. Fruit ripened and fell and was lost in the weeds, where hornets burrowed into it and came out too sticky to fly. Eventually Shelby noticed our father coming and going on his land and told him he could rent the spot. Since then, he began parking again on our lot, behind the shed. We'd been instructed to keep watch for tow trucks cruising the area.

With his elbow out the window, Dad called to us, "Hey, boys. Come on. We're going out for a while."

Levi and I climbed around the passenger seat into the foldout seats in back, and Carson sat up front, since his legs were too long to fit in back. He untucked the boomerang from his belt. The windshield wipers squealed and dragged black smears across the glass. The cab smelled warmly of stale cigarette smoke.

"Where we going?" Levi said.

"Where do you want to go?" Dad said. Levi shrugged and looked out the window. "We'll just go out for a bit." He put the truck in gear. "We'll go for a drive. My father took us out for a drive every Sunday." He looked at us in the rearview mirror and said, "All right," and then we drove off. As we passed the mill, Dad only said, "What a heartbreaker."

We brothers were just learning how to spend time around our father. After this many years of life, we'd become familiar only with the thud of his footsteps down the hall in the night and in the mornings a cup of cold coffee on the end table and the newspaper draped over a sofa arm. There had never been such a thing as a forty-hour workweek at the mill. After every shift, Dad and the other men blew off an hour or two at the Golden Nugget Tavern to prepare themselves for home life, whether the shift had ended at seven in the evening or seven in the morning.

Dad traded glances between us in the mirror and the road.

"Listen, boys," he said. "Your mother called today. Your grandfather died this morning."

We were quiet. Dad turned off toward the little city center.

"Does that mean Mom will be coming home?" I asked.

"Soon, Joel," Dad said. "She's not ready just yet. But she'll be back."

"She say when?" Levi said.

"No, but she won't be long." He noticed the old boomerang on Carson's lap. "What do you got there, Carson?"

"A boomerang. Found it behind the mill."

Dad looked at it for a few moments and nodded. "Think you're a little old for that?"

Carson shrugged.

"Why don't you give that to your brothers."

Carson tightened his grip on the toy and looked at our father.

"Go on," Dad said. He studied Carson's bruise for a moment.

Carson lowered his eyes and handed the boomerang to Levi, who took it and looked at me as though for direction. He sat with it in his lap, trying to hold it without touching it. We went on in silence.

"How about milkshakes, huh?"

He turned onto Second Street, which extended for no more than seven or eight blocks, with the Snowcap dead centered as if the whole town had been built around it. Dad rarely offered these sorts of luxuries, and even more rarely in the recent months of his unemployment, so we betrayed no reaction for fear that he had misspoken or that we had misunderstood. Dad parked alongside the curb and twisted the keys from the ignition and said, "Well, come on already." The ash-covered street was empty except for a few lonesome-looking men with their hands in their pockets walking as if they had somewhere to be. Above town the sky was the color of the place on a page where a penciled word has been poorly erased.

We tracked in gray footprints and a small gray gust, and a bell above the door sounded. I had been here before, but not for what felt like a very long time. The booths were empty and clean and the jukebox was playing and the walls were surfaced with wood paneling. There was a Coca-Cola glass-door refrigerator behind the counter full with sodas, and at the bottom, in a cardboard box, a pile of tomatoes.

"Ah," said a mustachioed man at the counter. "A few souls brave enough for doomsday weather." There was a girl behind him with an apron and a shy look about her, playing, it seemed, with some trinket in her pocket. She looked Carson's age.

"It'll take more than some ash to keep us home," Dad said.

"So it looks," the man said. "What'll you have?"

"Chocolate milkshakes. All around," he said. "Except not for me."

We sat at a booth by the window and followed the ash through the orange light of the streetlamps. We watched the second-floor windows of Main Street for the shapes of people turning behind the glass. Carson flicked away a flake of ash that had caught in Levi's lashes. The restaurant girl brought us three milkshakes on a yellow tray and said, "Here you are." Carson said thank you and watched her pass back behind the counter and disappear into the kitchen machinery. Carson stared for a while and then stirred his milkshake around.

"Talk to her, then," Dad told him.

Carson said, "Huh?"

"We see you watching her. Go talk to her."

"Why?" he said. "No." Then he bent down to his milkshake.

"Carson——" Dad crammed his knuckles into his pocket and pulled out some money.

"Actually, I would like a milkshake. Go order for me, would you? Just a small one. And don't you let her bring it over here. You wait there for it." Carson looked at the money and then took it. Dad caught his sleeve. "I want you to tell her your name. Okay? It doesn't matter if she doesn't tell you hers. You tell her yours." Carson paused and then he nodded and went off.

Dad and I watched him at the counter rubbing the back of his neck, and though we could hear his voice, we couldn't quite hear the words over the jukebox. She was redheaded and freckled and minia-ture in her proportions. I knew only that girls were pretty, but I hadn't any idea what to do with them yet. And then I noticed, and Dad after me, that Levi had picked a scab on his shin and he had a bit of blood on his fingers, which he was using to draw a stickman into the yellow plastic back pad to the booth.

"Hey, Levi," Dad said sternly.

Levi snapped to and looked at Dad with big eyes. He looked at the blood on his fingertips. Levi held them up for us to see, pushing his thumb and index finger together and pulling them apart, which made a small, tacky noise.

"Christ, Levi," Dad said. "People eat here." He sighed and massaged the bridge of his nose with his fingers. "All right. Go wash up. Get on." Levi hopped from the booth and dashed off to the bathroom. Dad scooted out of the booth and to the other side where Levi had sat.

"Dirty creature." He pulled a napkin from the dispenser and spat on it and scrubbed away Levi's little blood man. Then he looked at me and smiled wearily. We sat like this for a while, and I drank my milkshake.

"Where'd Carson get the shiner?" he asked.

I shrugged.

"He didn't say anything about it?"

"No."

"You ask him?"

"No."

He turned his attention to the window, where he watched the ash through his reflection.

"You might be the quietest kid in the world, Joel," he said.

I thought about this. "Maybe."

"Well, you shouldn't be, not if you can help it any. A guy needs to be able to demand things of the world. Otherwise—I don't know. Otherwise it'll roll right over you, and, well . . ."

I felt very small then, and yet I was thrilled even so by the wholeness of my father's attention. I said nothing because it seemed too much to begin speaking now.

"Maybe you shouldn't bother listening to me," Dad said. "I could've probably kept a few things to myself and been better for it. Maybe it's better to wish you'd said something than to regret saying something you shouldn't have. Maybe it'll all weigh on you just the same. Who knows? Never mind."

Then he looked at me for a while as I glanced around the room. Carson returned, put a milkshake in front of Dad, and said, "I told her my name."

"Did you?"

"She told me hers, too."

"And what was it?"

"It started with a 'J,'" he said, and smiled. He went to his milkshake.

"'J'?"

"She was quiet. It was a good name, but it was hard to hear exactly what she said."

Dad laughed and said, "That's something, I guess." And then he drank from his milkshake. When Levi returned, Dad made him show us his hands and his legs, and when Dad was satisfied with his cleanliness, he let him sit down. Levi was the first to ask about Mom again, and Dad said, "I told you, she didn't say when she'd be back. For all I know, it may be tonight. She may be on her way already. I can imagine that."

As we drove away, Dad told us about an old man who had refused to leave his house on Mount St. Helens and who had died there by a lake, which was vaporized along with him. He was one of the very few people killed by the eruption. Dad couldn't explain exactly why, but he said he admired the old fool. "It takes some sort of man," he said. "Got to believe it takes some certain sort of man to go down with his own like that." As they considered the man's motives and his final moments by the lake, I sat there wondering about what Dad had tried to tell me in the Snowcap—about the weight of words spoken and unspoken, which was not a weight I understood. And did that weight accumulate? I imagined then the weight Dad seemed to collapse with into a sofa, and the heaviness of his footsteps through the hall, and the hunch of his shoulders up a set of stairs. No, it did not make sense to me, so I sat there playing absently with my hands.

It was getting dark out and we didn't go straight home. Maybe this was because there was a repo man still snooping around or because we imagined the longer we stayed away, the more likely it was that Mom would be there when we arrived. Except we had nowhere else to go. As if by instinct, Dad drove us back by the paper mill. He parked in the empty lot, situated with our backs to the road, facing the broken shape of the mill hulking in the dark. He said, "I want to teach you boys something. Pay attention back there." He wrenched an elbow over the seat. "Here's the thing: you may be the best driver in the world, but your car can still fuck you. Or foul you up. Don't tell Mom I'm swearing. You need to know how to handle yourselves in an emergency." He put the pickup in neutral and stepped out and said into the cab, "Trade me, Carson."

Carson could drive manual. He used to move the car around to help Dad with chores. They stepped out into the dim lot and exchanged a few words in the headlights. Dad put a hand on Carson's shoulder and said a few words and looked directly into Carson's eyes, and then they parted and Carson climbed into the driver's seat.

"All right. What happens if you've got a stuck accelerator?"

Carson looked at Dad and then checked the pedals and said he didn't know.

"Imagine the truck is speeding up and up."

"All right."

"What's the first thing you do?"

Carson seemed unsure of the question, as though he were trying to discern our father rather than an answer, and as he sat there looking at him, Levi called out, "Hit the brakes."

"Right!" Dad shouted. "And then what? Say you speed up even

more." He waited and got tired and answered, "If you speed up when you hit the brake, it means you've been hitting the gas instead on accident. So take your feet off the pedals. And check—make sure the floormat hasn't wedged the pedal down."

"Okay," Carson said.

"You boys get that back there?" Dad said over his shoulder. "Now let's say there's a real malfunction with the throttle and you weren't just being dumbasses. So you keep going faster, even feet off the pedals. Put her in gear, Carson."

Carson put the shifter into first and waited.

"I shouldn't have said that—about being dumbasses," Dad said. "We all do dumbass things occasionally, and that's all right." He surveyed the lot and then he said, "Levi, I'm going to let you out. You see the pushcart there?"

"Yeah."

"Move that out of the way."

"Where do I move it?"

He stepped out so that Levi could exit from behind the seat and said, "I want you to push the cart as hard as you can that way." He pointed. Levi looked at him and smiled, and Dad said, "That's right. Hard as you can."

We laughed wildly when Levi set up behind the cart, which was loaded with a stack of copper piping, and heaved all his strength into it. The cart went rattling and caromed off a curb and let a few pipes loose and clattering into the other aisle of the lot. Levi was quiet, and then he held his arms up triumphantly, and Dad hooted.

"All right already," Dad shouted. "Get back in here!" Levi ran back and clambered in, and Dad said, "Okay, buckle up, then. Okay. Good, you're in first. In a moment here I want you to gun it. Get to the top end of second, you got that."

"Gun it?"

"Lead foot, Carson. And when I say so, throw her in neutral and start braking. You can do that?"

Carson paused and smiled and said that he thought so.

"And listen, when you brake, don't slam on it. You hit the brake all the way and we'll lock up. Once you've locked her up, we go skidding and there's no steering anymore. Keep your heel right there on the floor—good—and ease on just until the tires squeal. No howl though. Just a squeal. You ready? Don't think too much."

Carson, with his hands trembling on the wheel, nodded. I wanted to hug Levi in excitement. Dad clicked his seat belt in place.

Dad shouted, "First!" and Carson let out the clutch and hit the throttle. He shouted, "Second!" and Carson lurched into second. The lot, which had seemed so much larger in its emptiness, collapsed on us in the earlier dark. "Neutral!" Dad shouted. "Brake. Yes!" He pounded joyously on the dash and shouted, "Yes!" Levi was clapping and shouting in the dark of the cab as we came to rest in a cloud of ash, which lit up nearly white in the headlights, hung there for a moment, and dissipated.

Dad breathed deeply and regained himself and then, smiling over his shoulder at us, he asked, "And what if you can't get to neutral? What then?"

"Do we get to do it again?" Levi asked.

Carson was patting his fingers lightly on the wheel. "Then you have to kill the engine," he said.

Kill! What a word.

"That's right," Dad said. "We'll do it again. But now the clutch is out. The shifter is shit. Kill the engine. Get up to the top of second again. Levi, are you still buckled? Joel, make sure he's buckled."

I said he was.

"Carson, you know what it means when I say 'power brakes'?"

Carson looked at the brake pedal and shook his head.

"Means that, once the engine's off, the brakes lose most their juice. That's what the emergency brake is for." He patted beneath the dash at the emergency pedal and he slapped Carson's knee. "You see that?" Carson saw it. "When I tell you to kill it, hit the clutch, go to neutral, turn the ignition, and push the emergency brake. You won't be able to steer much with the engine off. This is a last resort. You got that?" Carson went over the steps once more aloud, then he pulled the truck around into the aisle as if it were a runway. We stared ahead into haze and felt our pulses clicking in our necks. Our mother was washing her father's deathbed sheets, and the truck already belonged to the bank, and ash was raining from the sky. "Go," Dad shouted. "Go, go, go!"

And we went.

THE FLIGHT INSTRUCTOR

I T HADN'T FULLY dawned on me yet, but I was finished flight instructing for good. I was still hanging around the Bend airport, working fuel service, thinking I'd get back to it sooner or later. The flight school hadn't placed me on suspension, but it would have raised eyebrows if I'd scheduled any student flights with an FAA investigation still hanging over my head. I thought I was only waiting for this mess to get straightened out, and dusting off my ego in the meantime. It hadn't occurred to me that my spirit had been dealt an unrecoverable blow. I was defeated. I was as good as walking around with my guts hanging out. Everyone else saw it, but no one had the heart to tell me. Denise, who managed the airport's main reception, as well as the flight school's administrative duties and coffee stand, had taken to hugging me every time I passed her desk, which was crowded with ceramic ducks. She couldn't help it. I'd see her scooting over to me in a daze, holding her arms out. And although we had no military affiliations, Manny, the chief pilot, gave me little salutes in the hall, before hurrying off in the opposite direction. Or Sadie Kent and Tim Dodd, fellow flight instructors, they called me out for a drink once, but I got too drunk and said who knows what and they didn't invite me out again. This uncommon kindness included even Drew Pretty, another flight instructor, and no friend to me. He gave me a lotto scratch card he'd bought for himself—a loser, incidentally—when he saw me looking at it. He left it in my mailbox without a note. All of these gestures I took as consolation for what I'd gone through, rather than, as it was intended: consolation for what I was going to go through still. By the end of the workweek, the FAA would fly out to Oregon to meet with me and look through the flight school records. We'd reach a conclusion then as to whether or not, and to what extent, I should be held accountable for the catastrophic destruction of one Cessna 152 and for the death of my flight student Liu Feng.

I got stuck on the FAA's email. I read it with every configuration of emphasis. *We* would reach a conclusion, as if I might unemploy myself out of good sense and spare them the trouble.

Liu Feng was a Chinese national. Most of my flight students and most of the flight school's students by the whole had been Chinese nationals, and now and then a rich old fellow who'd bought himself a plane he couldn't fly. A few years earlier China opened up airspace under three thousand feet to commercial use, and the Chinese government was still scrambling to make more pilots of their young men, exporting them to Podunk flight schools all across the States to start working toward commercial licenses. America is the place to do that. If you fly international, you have to fly with some English.

Before the death of my student and the loss of the dinky Cessna we trained on, I'd kept a twice-a-week routine of driving the Chinese cadets to the supermarket for toilet paper and ramen cups and the basic things they needed to survive. It put me into a paternal frame of mind about them, although some of the bunch were a few years older than me. None of them had driver's licenses or cars or their wits about them in this foreign land. They'd all arrived stateside fairly bewildered, with only a few words of English and just a couple changes of clothes. It was a central responsibility of my job, running the cadets on errands. I hadn't expected that when I signed on as an instructor. I thought mostly I'd be flying.

The last time I took Liu Feng and the cadets on such an errand run, they were all pulling their hair out. They had check rides coming up, which they'd have to pass to continue through the next units of their training and which they were all hoping to pass the first go-round. A check ride is really just a progress check and feels much like the test for a driver's license. If a pilot fails one, he only has to put in some practice and take the ride again until he passes. But I've pulled my hair out over check rides too, so I sympathized. I had the cadets in the airport shuttle, a dog-shit passenger van, which I drove around like a bumper car, as if it might impress someone how little I cared for something that wasn't mine anyway. We went to Walmart, rather than Safeway, this time. Walmart, I'd already learned, added another twenty minutes to an errand run, because Walmart had a sporting goods department and guns. The cadets loved the guns. They liked taking pictures of themselves with the assault-style rifles. Liu Feng posed holding two AR-15s—this is when Walmart still sold AR-15s. He looked to me and said, "Rambo," and I agreed, although Rambo didn't smile so much. I made him send me a copy of the photo so that I could make it appear on my cell phone when he called to schedule flights, although my students really only sent texts, so that they could translate at their own pace. Then a sour-faced attendant with a heap of facial hair grew tired of us and asked if we were serious customers or not.

The Civil Aviation Administration of China put all the cadets up in the same apartment complex, and the rest, as far as their well-being was concerned, was up to me and the flight school. It was the sort of facility where divorced dads go to finish out the rest of their days and do no harm: furnished one-bedrooms and little concrete patios; where the bachelors sat awaiting their children's visitations, hiding the ashtrays beneath a bush by the door once a week. I come from a tradition of divorced men myself—my father, and his father before him—which left me little hope for myself in the arena of romance, but hope I did anyway, still feeling that it'd be some hidden villainy in me in the end that would undo everything I wanted, an inward, God-given badness. So the Chinese cadets had moved into the divorced-dad complex as a great ruckus of life and sound and brought to the place a youthful shine—the hopeful urgency of being young men still, but not for too much longer. I drove them the way home and thought, these guys, my hopeful cadets, they had to get out of their heads. They were bottoming their hearts out with worry. I passed the complex by and kept going.

The cadets swiveled in their seats. "We're taking the town, boys," I called over my shoulder. I didn't understand a word of what the cadets shouted about as we went, but they were excited, I could tell, and now and then they slapped my arm or touched the back of my head to be sure I felt included. We were all doing what we loved. We were pilots. It was how we introduced ourselves.

I had the idea to take the cadets to the bar, then realized I'd gotten myself in over my head. Two or three of the cadets sat drinking sodas or sipping beers at the table, minding their own business, but I found a few drinkers in the group who were willing to humor me. None of this struck me as a misuse of my authority because I didn't believe I had any. We were picking up the pace quickly and effortlessly enough that I hadn't noticed the night beginning to career. Min Li and Zhang Jun got their hands on the darts and only rarely managed to hit the dartboard. I thought, if someone doesn't stop them soon, this will get hazardous. I sat in high anticipation, wondering who would put a halt to it. By then it seemed I was doing a bit of a career, too. I'd come into possession of a hat that wasn't mine. Michael Feng had arrived to the Foosball game uninvited, but not especially unwelcome. Troy Yang was trying to sample cocktails. Liu Feng—no relation to Michael Feng, it turned out, just a common name, and, I hoped, a common mistake—he'd become my main guy. Everyone knew it because I often said so. He stuck around with me, laughing wherever I pointed. Zhang, for instance, was shouting happily at Min, who had a dart in his leg, though, at this point in the night, it looked like Zhang had a dart in his leg also. It struck us all as a miraculous coincidence. They compared their legs side by side.

Somewhere in these shenanigans we called Drew Pretty to come meet us if he wanted. Half of these attendant students were his, after all. I didn't care for Drew Pretty. He exasperated the whole flight school staff, except for Denise, who cherished everyone. Drew took every chance to tell you things you already knew. He made a show of concern when he arrived at the bar.

"They're all going nuts," Drew said. "Goddamn, Eddie."

"They really are, aren't they?"

"Especially you, too," he said. "If he saw this, Manny's eyes would pop in his head. You know this is where Manny goes drinking with his cop buddies. Did you think about that?"

I had thought about that. It hadn't struck me as important, and it still didn't. Manny wasn't here, and neither were his cop buddies. At least not in uniform, but I supposed they wouldn't be in uniform. Manny had been a cop for just a little while as a young man, but he still enjoyed talking that talk. Then I saw Liu was showing Drew something on his cell phone, which seemed to have a bad effect on Drew's mood.

"The hell, Eddie? I thought we said no more Walmart? He's got two machine guns."

"Come on, Liu," I said. "You're spoiling it."

"AR-15s," Liu said. "What? Sorry, sorry."

"And you invite me out here just when everyone's too drunk to even remember me being here," Drew said.

"That was Liu's idea," I said. "Liu decided we had to get you out here too. We were just warming up for you."

"It was Michael's idea," Liu corrected me. Then he apologized again.

Thankfully, Drew could get drunk as quick as a puppy. I bought him a first round, and within a half hour he'd grown bored of his complaining and instead brutalized the jukebox with the whole Pearl Jam discography. He sang to us over our drinks—a surprisingly capable singer, really—jutting out his jaw in such a way that made me want to ash a cigarette in it. The bartender hated us. He said my friends were out of hand. My friends, I repeated, yes! I was a pilot, I told him. I had friends all over the globe—America, China, everywhere. It was at this moment that Drew came out of the bathroom and said we had to go. He said someone had kicked a hole in the bathroom wall and everyone thought it was him. Then Drew went outside and vanished graciously.

Per the bartender's suggestion, I ushered the cadets out and into the shuttle, then stared at the ignition for a while, feeling especially touched. The cadets hadn't let me pick up my tab. They waved me away with an affectionate play of irritation, in which same spirit, if there is a God, I hope he will come to meet me at the big holy door. Then I imagined it'd make big news if an American CFI killed seven Chinese nationals in a drunk shuttling accident. We ended the night with a two-mile walk back to the apartment complex.

Not since I was in college have I wandered home drunk with so many friends in the orange light of streetlamps overhead. I managed to return all seven of my charges, though not without some help from the two sober pilots who went on ahead, tired but in good humor, to lead the way. Liu invited me in and invited me to get situated on his sofa. There we consumed a convict's last-meal's worth of Chinese snack foods, which had been mailed to him by a loved one as a reminder of home. He came to me with these treats spilling from his arms, handing me one after the next, little wrapped candies or puffs or chews, and he laughed over my wonderment of each. I turned the treats around in the lamplight to see their colors.

Liu brought his laptop over and opened his Facebook, and the words were all Chinese characters. His desk was stacked with flight books and manuals. A well-annotated English-to-Chinese dictionary lay open, and a model of what looked to be an F-14 stood in mid-construction. I was happy and in the mood to be astonished. Liu Feng sat himself beside me on the sofa and showed me pictures of people he knew from home. He told me their names, and waited for me to nod in recognition. There was Mom and Dad. There was Girlfriend or Ex-Girlfriend maybe, I asked, but it seemed from his hasty expression of repulsion that we were looking at his sister or cousin or I didn't know who. We were drunk and speaking different languages again. Then Liu scrolled past a photo of himself in his aviators, looking stoic in the cockpit of a Cessna and the sun going red in the air. I told him to scroll back, scroll back, but he was embarrassed. Technically, pilots aren't encouraged to fuss with cell phones and cameras in flight, but we'd all taken pictures like that. I had. What was the use in being an airplane pilot if no one saw you flying the airplane? I said, "Yeah, that's cool. That's undeniably cool."

Liu shrugged and smiled with some embarrassment still, and he said, "Very cool, yeah." Then he scrolled on and showed me a picture of an American bikini model pressing herself lustily against a dirt bike, a red Honda. I told Liu if I'd been born next door to him in China, we would have been friends all on our own, even without this pilot business to string us together. He smiled and waited for me to finish talking. Then he gave me a blanket and brought a glass of water to the table beside the sofa.

THE NEXT DAY, after a grueling walk to retrieve the shuttle, I took Michael Feng, then Liu Feng, on our scheduled flights, and nearly threw up twice. We'd meant to practice stall and recovery maneuvers, and work on the cadets' verbal communications with Air Control, but we took it easy instead and said no more than we had to. Neither of the Fengs had much more color in their faces than I did. Michael got the plane up and down just fine, but Liu bounced his landing hard. That's a strain on an aircraft's structural integrity. It had me feeling around for my stomach. Manny came shouting over the radio.

"Who the hell did I just see dribble my Cessna on the tarmac like a fucking basketball?"

Liu got teary, and I felt mournful about myself. I said, "Dammit, Liu. What are you doing here? You've gotta get better. You just have to."

He looked at the dash controls frantically as if he might find an answer written somewhere. Then he turned to me with his humiliation. I didn't know where to begin. When we killed the engine at the open hangar, Liu sat for a while in the cockpit, holding his headset in his lap.

"Look," I said. "We'll get you there, okay? I don't know how yet. But at least we're down, yeah?" I told Liu what I told any of my bad landers. There were only two ways back to ground: in one piece or many pieces, and we were in one piece and that was a start. "Your check ride will have to go better than this one," I said. "You can only improve from here."

The next week Drew kept his distance from me around the airport, which I noted first as pleasant, thinking perhaps Drew—after his bar antics the other night—was capable of embarrassment after all. Later his avoidance began to strike me as conspicuous. I hadn't heard from Liu in a minute either, and that worried me suddenly. Eventually I caught on. Liu had failed his check ride. It'd been Drew who administered the ride and Drew who failed him.

I HAD LIU run me through the check ride, moment by moment. Right after takeoff, Drew started picking at him. "Manny probably would have failed you for just that," Drew had said. Liu hadn't made a show of checking the weather conditions because it was very apparently blue and windless in every direction. What else is there to say about that sort of weather except, dear God, and dear Air Traffic Control, isn't the day a beauty? Liu was beat before he began. Instructors are not to speak during check rides, except to issue instruction, otherwise you're only getting into the student's head. Drew knew that but would do anything to feel smarter than another pilot, even student pilots. I suspect Liu might have failed no matter what, but having someone like Drew picking at you, with a mean, pettiness of spirit—that part I had trouble stomaching. Later in the flight, Liu neglected to make a perfunctory call to Air Control, then flubbed another call, and Drew said again, Manny would have failed him for that on the spot. And things went on that way, Drew butting in, especially in troubles communicating with Center, until Drew had enough to fail Liu himself.

"Failing that, that, everything," Liu told me.

"But how was your landing?" I asked, although it didn't matter.

"Also not good."

He shook his head.

I told Liu plenty of perfectly good pilots had failed check rides. Even I had failed a check ride once. My nerves caught me at the wrong time, and I nearly tried to land on the taxiway before the instructor yanked on the controls. But that wasn't a story I wanted floating around the flight school, so I kept it to myself. I sat beside Liu scratching my head, then told him there were surely plenty of perfectly capable pilots out there who'd failed a check ride. More important, the CAAC, I reminded him, was paying for his training. So just pay to take the test again. A failed check ride left no mark of consequence on a pilot's record, just the ego. I said I'd be sure he flew with Sadie Kent next time around, who didn't overly care for me, but whose judgment and ability I respected. All through this Liu nodded and nodded but kept his gaze downturned at his sneakers. "This is nothing," I said. "This is just a minor embarrassment." But even as I told him so, I felt my heart hardening against him, like letting a man drown.

I left Liu sitting there while I cut out the back way between the hangars because I was afraid that if I ran into Drew Pretty I'd say something that'd curse us both to hell.

The week following his botched check ride, I saw Liu Feng was scheduled on a solo flight and I signed off on it. I thought, good for Liu, back on the horse. He's putting in the work. When I failed my check ride, for a counterpoint, I wasted a couple weeks feeling low and indignant about myself before I'd recovered enough confidence to schedule a solo flight. Liu's takeoff was almost a beauty for once, deliberate, as if he'd made his mind up about something. He lifted like a kite on an easy, steady updraft, a long down-rolling lawn below, and a choreography of irrigation beyond that, tidy little rivers in their concrete luges—I never really knew how to speak my love for the physical world until I called myself a pilot, and then suddenly I felt I had permission. I watched Liu from the hangar bay, working a dirty rag over my greasy hands. Sometimes I can still summon goose bumps at a clean takeoff and even better for a clean landing. I have managed to keep it sacred. So here I am, saying a prayer of thanks to the bird gods of flight. I watched with a sharp, gut-filling force of gratitude as Liu Feng climbed the pale distance and shrunk from sight.

The next morning Manny informed me that Liu had veered off his charted course immediately after reaching altitude, then he nosed out westward, raising hell from Air Traffic as he punched through PDX airspace without a word about clearance. And then, we were told, once he'd reached the Pacific Ocean, he opened the cabin door and stepped out. The plane continued without its pilot for over one hundred miles into the blue nowhere and left no trace.

MANNY MET ME in his office, which was strewn with photos in homely frames he'd made himself. Photos of planes and fish. I asked if Manny knew what the hell happened and he said, yeah, he knew what happened. Just two days after Liu's failed check ride, the CAAC issued his recall. Most American pilots in training, after failing a check ride, will give it another try a few weeks later, once they've raised the funds again and put in some extra practice. Apparently the CAAC decided Liu Feng lacked the disposition at his first strike. They summoned him back home to—I didn't know what goes on—work in a factory? I said, I hadn't heard any of that. No one told me.

"Yeah, me neither," Manny said.

"China should have told us at least."

"It's a mess, Eddie. It shouldn't have landed on you."

"No one told me," I said again. They were the only words I knew for minutes at a time.

"I know," Manny said. "Hell. It's a mess."

"I saw Liu had a solo on the schedule and I was only happy about it."

Manny had nothing left to offer me in the way of information or sympathy and he started fumbling at his desk as if he'd misplaced something crucial, which was his way of asking me to leave. Like my fellow flight instructors, post–Liu's death, Manny treated me with pity and tenderness, but also a squeamish, carefully kept distance. I always liked Manny. He showed me my usefulness once. I wanted more from him now than he could provide me, and I pitied us both. I told him thanks for nothing, which is the way we always spoke to one another, and left for home.

Drew Pretty was standing there in the parking lot in the cold, stiff morning when I came out from Manny's office. I saw his pink face and it occurred to me suddenly how much I hated him. I hated him so much I felt religious about it. Drew must have seen this realization animate my face. He saw me and then made himself look like he was two feet tall. I stepped by him, then he trailed after me at a safe distance into the parking lot.

"That about Liu Feng in there?" Drew asked. I tried to ignore him, but he didn't mind. "What'd Manny say about it?"

"He said Liu killed himself and took a Cessna with him."

"Oh shit."

"You already heard that."

"Yeah," Drew said. "But shit. Liu, he seemed like a good dude."

Just to see how it sounded aloud, I told Drew I ought to haul off and punch him in the gut.

"Me? What did I do? Is the FAA coming?"

"They're coming to turn every stone over."

"What did I do? Did I really come up?"

Then I surprised myself by lying. I told Drew I'd heard all about the check ride before Liu went and killed himself, which was true, and that I discussed it all with Manny, which wasn't true. I didn't say anything about Drew in there. I avoided mention of the check ride altogether for the fear that the quality of my instruction might be mentioned next. "Liu told me you were picking at him the whole time," I said. "Talking trash. So I gave Manny, you know, a full accounting of events."

137

"I wasn't picking on him!" Drew's voice came out in squawks.

"I should just haul off and punch you in the gut."

"Did Manny say anything about me? Liu couldn't talk to Control, Eddie. He couldn't get a command out. What was I supposed to do?"

I took my keys from my pocket and looked around. It was dry and frigid-cold and all the moisture had turned to snow wisps, snaking between our legs then over the blacktop. Drew told me again that he hadn't done anything, and then I walloped him low in the belly. He clenched over and puked on his shoes, and a little on my shirtsleeve, which frightened me. Drew stood doubled over and heaving for a while as I wiped the vomit from my arm onto my pant leg.

"No one's ever hit me before," he said, gasping.

"I've never hit anyone," I said. It amazed me how effortlessly possible it was to haul off and punch someone as hard as you could. I was worried I'd hurt him and at the same time disappointed that I wasn't capable of more destruction. It made me feel sick and it made me want to punch him again, harder, somewhere more vital, before my conscience caught up with my adrenaline. I might have, but Drew started moaning. "Fuck, Eddie, my shoes," he said. He had a hand over his face. "My best shoes."

I stooped into my little Honda, and when I drove off, Drew was still there, scrubbing vomit from his shoes with a palmful of snow dusting.

I THOUGHT THE first FAA meeting would either leave me exonerated completely or doomed, but more or less nothing happened. The two nights before, I'd hardly slept. The FAA wanted a complete record of

all my flight logbooks, which the Bend flight school was always insti-
tutionally lax about keeping. I stayed up nights forging my records. I'd
kept names and dates, for the most part, but I had to fabricate some
of the particulars. The school's other instructors, just at the whiff of
the FAA coming, stayed up nights supplementing their own records,
too. Manny spent one or two in his office himself. Denise made up his
sofa with a blanket she kept in her car. Manny and Denise very much
loved one another, I think, but never made anything of it. They're both
the sort to confess their tenderest affections only at the gravestone.

The FAA in the flesh were just two regular middle-aged men. They
were concerned, they said, that I'd taken on so many students with
whom I couldn't communicate so well. I told them I just took whoever
the flight school gave me, and they said they were taking this into ac-
count. One agent took point and wielded his notepad, I thought, like
an instrument of psychological torture. With his one hand, he wrote
down my responses slowly and carefully, and with his other, he held
up a finger until he was ready for me to proceed. What lengths had I
gone to prepare my students' English, he asked, as in, had I made any
FAA and IACO language resources available to them? I asked what the
IACO language resources were. They traded a look between themselves and seemed disheartened. They did agree, though, that it was
an error of grave consequence that I hadn't been informed about the
CAAC's decision to recall the pilot in question. They said they would
figure out what happened there. In the meantime, I could proceed
with my duties as usual and we'd have another meeting soon to reach
a final conclusion on the matter once they'd had a chance to peruse
all the records. What struck me most about the whole thing was how
scarce Liu was in the conversation. They never mentioned the suicide

at all. I was waiting, but no one said a word about it. It was as if we were talking about a theoretical pilot, a man who'd never lived.

A few weeks later and I still hadn't resumed my regular duties. Instead, I picked up night shifts refueling airplanes on the fuel line because I wasn't sleeping either. The season's first real snow had just dumped on us out of nowhere, and then the first ice cover just as quickly, so that the wind skated it all over without disturbing a thing. The clouds trailed off in the late evening and a dim, lunar glow shined on the ice. In the distance, another weather front was rising darkly. I'd just finished plowing the tarmac, when two perfectly unrelated, calamitous things happened to me. Because they happened so near together, one right after the next, I have twined them in my memory as part and parcel of the one incomprehensible, cosmic design that I seemed to be swept up in.

The first calamity came to me as a phone call. I removed a glove and rummaged my phone from my pocket and then suddenly there was Liu Feng lit up in my hand. There was his picture on my cell phone with the two AR-15s propped on his hips. I'd forgotten the photo by then. Liu's big stupid grin, smiling back to me from beyond the living light. I sat on the idling plow in the biting wind. Terror took me. I put the phone to my ear and waited.

Then a voice said, "Hello? Eddie?"

It was Michael Feng. So claimed the voice at least. I wasn't right away convinced of anything. It would take more than reason to undo the horror in me. He wanted to know if I'd schedule any flights with him soon—which sounded like something Michael might ask—or if he should start marking Sadie Kent as his instructor on record from now on. He'd been texting me for a while and I'd been neglecting those texts. That was also true. All of this he said gently, very gently. I asked him, "But why do you have Liu Feng's picture?"

"Liu Feng?"

"Your picture is Liu Feng's picture," I said.

"It's Michael Feng," he said. "Not Liu Feng. Michael."

"But you got his picture on my phone," I said. By now it had begun to seem remotely possible that, when I'd programmed Liu Feng's number with Liu's photo, I'd accidentally assigned it to the other Feng in my contacts. Michael was silent on the other end for some time as I performed these insane calculations. He thought I was crazy. I considered trying to convince him otherwise, but couldn't see the use. "Sadie Kent is a good pilot," I said eventually. "You can tell the guys that. One of the best. Well, she's better at the communication stuff anyway."

This, too, Michael met with a period of silence. Michael and Liu Feng, as I already said, weren't brothers, but that mistaken presumption had left a sort of impression on me that they were close and that if I owed Liu anything, then it was bequeathed to Michael now. But I didn't know a thing about what those cadets did outside the cockpit or the shuttle van. Michael and Liu might have known only as much about each other as I knew about either of them, which was next to nothing. I realized I'd been quiet for a long time. Michael said, "We talk about you, Eddie. We say, we hope you come back, but if not, that's okay too."

"All right, Michael," I said. "Thanks for that. Listen, I can call Sadie. I'll tell her you're coming her way."

We traded goodbyes and I went to warm myself inside, and before I could make sense of what had happened and how I felt about it, the second calamity happened. I stood at the lobby window, looking at my dark cell phone screen, at a reflection of my face downturned and scrunched up in the jowls, when I saw a pair of headlights take the road. I looked up. I watched for a while, then I decided it was a police SUV.

The police turned into the airport lot, and I thought, they've come for me. I realized ever since Liu died, I'd been like a fugitive in my heart. Two officers stepped out and removed a third man from the back of the SUV. This third fellow clomped forth, between the pair of officers, over the new snow and ice, giving stiltedly beneath him, and so it took me a moment to notice how drunk he was and then another moment to see that it was Drew Pretty. They brought him through the door, wasted and empty in his eyes. The first officer stomped the snow from his boots and then introduced himself as Officer Stanton. "I expect you're already acquainted with Drew here."

The officer said they'd found Drew a bit off the road, that he'd had a bit too much to drink. Why they were telling me this, I had no idea. Why they had come to the airport, I didn't know that yet either. The suspense nearly killed me. Well, the trouble was, the one officer said eventually, as early as it was for snow, no one had put their snow tires on yet, and the weather had set off a night of simultaneous disasters. Fender benders, more than worth counting. Slips and falls and broken wrists, a hip. A poor old woman bloodied her nose against the steering wheel in a traffic collision. An even more urgent call had just come in, the one officer said, a ways farther out of town. The officer gave no more information as to this more urgent matter.

"It's a real mess, just farther out of town," he said. "But meanwhile we got Drew here with us. Gotta get him back to the station with us to book him. When Drew tells us he works at the airport—and we're going that way anyway—we figured we'd give Manny a call, ask him if we can't drop Drew off for a little while, let him hang around the lounge until we're through, then we pick him up on our way back to the station."

"Now's the part," the other officer said, "where we ask a favor of you."

I looked at Drew, but all through this he didn't say a word, nor did he seem to register a word that was said, not even perking up at mention of his name. He wasn't in handcuffs, but it was plain that he was a goner.

"All I need is for you to let Drew sit there. We'll be back for him in a couple hours," the officer said. "Tell me this, what is it that Drew does at the airport? Does he work fuel service with you? We didn't get much out of him."

"He's a flight instructor," I said. "Me too. I'm just moonlighting."

"He's a pilot?"

I said he was, and the officer rubbed his eyes heavily and looked to his partner. "Hell," he said. He thought about that for a moment and then shook it off. "Well, then, you two—are you work buddies, then?"

Drew shocked me by speaking. "Eddie hates my guts," he said.

The officers gave each other another look and nodded and seemed satisfied.

"Except, say he gets it in his head to run off?" I said.

"Drew won't try anything funny, will you, Drew?" the one officer said. "If he does, I suggest you strongly advise him against the notion."

The second officer said, "I got his keys. Drew, I got your keys," and then, most shocking to me of all, the officer called Stanton knelt to the carpet and untied Drew's boots. He told Drew to step on out, then he rose with Drew's boots held in his one hand and looked at them, then to me. "There," he said. "In case he gets any stupid ideas in his head. Ho! You see this, Drew? Got your boots, okay? I'll bring them back, okay?" Then he asked me to thank Manny for them. Drew looked on limply into middle space. With that, the officers stepped back out into the cold and drove off opposite the way they'd come, casting a ring of red from their taillights on the snow as they went. Drew and I stood in the lobby vestibule, Drew in his socks, standing in a sop of snowmelt.

I LED DREW to the lounge, although he knew where it was. Drew sat on the sofa. I turned the TV on. We watched the local news for twenty minutes before we spoke at all. I asked if they'd Breathalyzed him. Drew shook his head. "Have to do it at the station later."

I thought about this. We both, and probably the officers, too, had been fretting about the consequence of a DUI on a young pilot's record. If a pilot had already made captain at a big airline, he was still relatively golden. If, on the other hand, a pilot got a DUI before making captain, chances are he'd never make it that far.

"You know," I said, "it might be, by the time they get you there, your blood alcohol level could be down to legal again."

"Don't think so."

"They even took your shoes. I can't believe that."

Drew wiggled his toes. "It was those same shoes, too."

"Which?"

"Ones I barfed on. Back when you coldcocked me in the gut."

"Oh," I said, "right."

"I cleaned them like brand-new, but God just doesn't want me having those shoes. And for another thing, he doesn't want me being a pilot, I don't think," Drew said, as if it were nothing. "I don't think God wants you for a pilot either, Eddie."

I told Drew I'd been entertaining a similar feeling, and then he looked at me with a smile, a pitiful one.

"You never liked me, did you, Eddie?" he said. "I could tell you didn't, even at the start. You get this idea in your head that people are just razzing you and they'll come around, but no."

"It's true, I guess," I said. "I make my mind up about people pretty early on."

Then Drew leaned over, folding his arms on his knees, and stared at my shoes dolefully. "I keep looking at your shoes, don't I? Look nice. Mmm, those shoes, man!" He laughed. "Ah, but I actually wish you'd told me your mind was made up. Then I could have just not worried about it."

"Listen, I'm not giving you my shoes."

"Yeah, I won't ask," Drew said, but he kept staring at my shoes anyway.

We watched the TV for a while, news coverage of Bend's downtown stretch. People were angry at the weather, looking ridiculous, slip-sliding and pink-faced in their puffy coats. We sat quiet like this until halfway through the commercial break, when Drew roused back to life. "I just had a fantasy," he said, "where I knocked you over the head and took those shoes off you. Made my escape. Took your car keys, too. I drove off in your car, out of this whole mess, drove right out of Bend and kept going. Maybe I finish up my flight hours in Montana with the moose. Except, different the second time around because this time everyone sees I got something to offer and I'm not so bad. I'll fit right in with the big Montanans. Next thing I'm a real pilot, flying a Q400, then the 747, Alaska maybe. Next thing after that," he said, holding up his empty hand, "a pretty woman is admiring my uniform and she flat out marries me. She'll be the kindest woman I ever met and she thinks I look so sharp in my uniform, she decides, right then and there, she wants to heap all that kindness on me for the rest of her life and never changes her mind. Picture that, Eddie. And all of it starts with something as easy as cracking you over the head with one of Denise's ducks." Drew looked at Denise's ceramic ducks. I was silent all through this. I watched Drew's inner life pouring from his mouth, and his future, which might have been spot-on for all I knew, and I felt as though he might tell me what happens to me in the end while he'd struck his connection with the winking mystery of the universe, but he didn't. "Or you could go along with it, maybe," he said. "You could tell the police someone cracked you over the head, but we only make it *look* like someone cracked you over the head."

I asked Drew how we'd make it look like someone cracked me over the head, and Drew thought about this, then shifted himself on the sofa to face me directly. "I guess I'd still have to crack you over the head a little bit," he said, "but we'd be doing it together. No meanness about it."

"And what about my car?"

"Your car would become my car. It goes to Montana with me. That's the beauty of it. No one would suspect a thing."

"Drew, I see what you're getting at," I said. "I actually do. But I still see me staying in my shoes tonight."

"Okay, well, Eddie, you know what? The other thing I wanted to tell you is, Liu, he wasn't ever gonna pass that check ride, whether it was me or someone else flying with him. I've been thinking on it. Liu, a good dude or whatever, but God definitely didn't want him for a pilot."

"I don't feel like getting into that."

"So go on and coldcock me again."

"I won't. I just won't get into it."

Drew looked at me wildly. Suddenly I had a sort of tenderness for him. "Let me ask you something," I said. "I keep thinking. Your check rides—"

"Listen, Eddie. All I said to Liu up on the check ride was the truth about how bad he was doing. I'm committed to not feeling any worse about it." He held his arms out, not as a boast for violence, but as if to say, see, look at me, drunk and shoeless on the sofa.

"Not the check rides you've instructed," I said. "I mean your own personal check rides."

"So what?"

"Did you fail any?"

"Me? Hell no," Drew said. He made himself look indignant. "I passed all my check rides like you or Sadie or fuckin' Dodd or any of the rest of you."

"I failed a check ride," I said. It was easy to say. I hoped he'd think less of me for saying it. "My first one at Top Flyt."

"I never failed any check ride, Eddie, and you won't get me to say I did."

"I almost tried to land on the taxiway."

Drew laughed. "Well, Manny would have failed you for that one, I guess."

"He did."

"Lucky you weren't at the whims of the CAAC."

"I've been thinking that, too."

"The damn CAAC. You know, at first I thought, shoot, Liu didn't have to take the Cessna with him, now did he? I liked number eleven best. But now I've been thinking, actually, maybe I'd do it that way too. Riding good old number eleven, one last flight into the sunset, like a fucking cowboy, ha."

"I don't want to talk romantic about it."

"Ah, I'm just talking drunk about it. You can coldcock me and I won't even feel it this time. Actually, I wouldn't even mind it."

I said again that I wouldn't, but Drew kept daring me to coldcock him—that was his way of saying it—and it turned into something like a drunken singsong after a few verses, *coldcock me, so go on and coldcock me, Eddie.* The Liu conversation already had me feeling itchy with panic, so I stepped out for a while. I left Drew alone in the lounge and was grateful to receive a call-ahead from a couple pilots—for a refuel and one for a weekend arrival. I hadn't expected any customers at that hour, or in that weather, and suddenly I hoped my plow job had been the real thing and not just a show of plowing. The first pilot in his Bonanza made easy work of it. He swooped down from the north, from an empty sky, obliterating the moon-quiet, and taxied round to meet me. He took a cup of coffee. I sprayed the Bonanza's wings with deicer, and then right on its tail, another pilot showed up for the arrival, carrying a load of loud corporate guys for a bachelor party in the mountains. The pilot had me clean his Citation's bathroom, as was my duty when requested. The bachelors gathered their things and the pilot sat in the cockpit, calling back to me, saying he hoped it wasn't too messy in there. He had the bathroom cleaned not so long ago; I was doing God's work, so on.

Thinking back on all this, I have wondered if I wasn't giving Drew a chance to run off. I would have denied it at the time, but then again, I was really taking my time with that lavatory—I was perfecting that plastic toilet—and then even well after I'd taken the bachelors and their luggage to a taxi awaiting them out front, I lingered outside by the hangar for a windbreak, wishing Drew to disappear.

And so Drew had. I found the TV playing to an empty room. It was past midnight. I checked the front door and I saw nothing in the way of footprints leaving, except for what the cops had left earlier. The bathroom was empty. At the building's side entrance, I found what I was looking for: broken snow and ice. So he'd attempted the unadvisable after all. A few steps in and it looked as though Drew took a minor tumble, but got back up, as if he'd started a snow angel and then someone had called his name.

I spent much of this night confused by a number of things, and I worried that maybe I was drunk too, although I'd had nothing to drink. Hardly had I left the airport than I had to stop and scratch my head. It looked very much as though there were two trails I was following, two distinct tracks trudging off in the night, keeping four or so feet abreast of the other. I couldn't puzzle it out. Whose were the second prints, I didn't know. I imagined the ghost of Liu Feng, leading Drew into the frozen night. The two trails cut down the side of the tarmac and then veered off into the open, up a low rise in the country. The other side of that, if you kept on another half mile or so, was the highway, but not before an irrigation canal. You'd have to be an Olympic long jumper to clear a canal, and even then it was not particularly feasible in those blizzard conditions. Drew was the shape of a giant almond and drunk and wouldn't make it more than half a foot from earth in any weather.

The snow was up almost to my knees, and the icy top layer made it hell to get through, breaking through again and again each step. I felt it in my hip flexors and faintly in my conscience, because like anyone else, I always feel sad to ruin fresh snow. Once I'd reached the canal, I thought I'd know for certain where Drew had turned next: either southwest toward the highway or northeast, deeper into the sparse juniper country and occasional cattle land. Honestly, it occurred to me only then, as I pursued his trail, that I was partly responsible for Drew's acts of self-endangerment. I'd lied to him, hadn't I? The FAA had no interest in Drew. No one cared about Liu's check ride. I'd meant the lie to bear cruel fruits, hadn't I, and here they were borne more plumply magnificent than I could have hoped. Drew was the only person concerned about Drew, besides Denise, who's inexhaustible powers of affection were both pathological and indiscriminate.

As I mulled all this over, the twin trails seemed suddenly to end some fifteen yards from the canal. There was a smattering plod of footprints where perhaps Drew had paced about in his moment of reckoning—consulting his mysterious escort, or pleading—before, it seemed, he disappeared completely. Was it my turn to vanish next, I wondered? Alternatively, I had the fantasy that I'd return to town to find myself the last man on earth.

It was a shamefully long time that it took me to understand, the second pair of footprints were also Drew's—one track as he made this way into the snowy waste, and one track retreating to the airport. And that's where I found him: in the airport, not in the lounge where

I'd left him, but two doors down the hall in Manny's office, fetal on the sofa and shawling himself in the bedding Denise had tucked in the desk's bottom drawer. I saw his socks melting on the floor and his fucked-up feet poking out from beneath the blanket. His toes were bloated and shiny as if he'd dipped them into a pool of hornets.

I said, "Drew, your feet are fucked-up. Wake up." But he held his eyes closed tightly now, held the blanket tight over his shoulders. I touched the worst of the toes and it felt like the toe of a wax sculpture, as if I could snip it off without disturbing him in the least.

The police station gave me the answering machine. A few tries and I gave up calling. I took Drew's pink feet and wrapped them in my jacket and sat with them in my lap, nestling them in the heat of my groin. I wasn't sure if Drew was supposed to sleep or not, but I couldn't stop him, so he slept and we waited like that for the police who never came. Whatever disaster had taken the officers away had not returned them, or else they had forgotten us. Drew and I sat like this until a dazzling, snow-gleamed morning arrived in the windows. He woke at first light and said his feet hurt him some, removing them from my lap with embarrassment, which I took as an encouraging sign.

No police officers came calling, then or later. No one ever said anything again about Breathalyzing Drew, or returned his boots, or his keys. I had to drive him out to his apartment for a spare key and a pair of sneakers, then back to his truck. Snow was still heavy on the roads. Here and there cars sat abandoned at the shoulder, nosed into snowbanks. We reached his truck and Drew stepped out and looked off into the distance where the canal lay far out of sight still. "Last night, I really thought I'd almost made it back to my truck," he said.

He looked back to me. "But I wasn't even close." Then he closed my passenger door and left.

I TAKE IT Manny heard part of the story from one of the officers, but without an arrest, he let Drew keep on at the Bend flight school anyway, walking around on ten perfectly good toes. Drew pretended the night never happened and said nothing more about Montana, but then life did one of its big turnarounds on me anyway. In the space of half a year, I was the one in Montana, and Drew never went anywhere. He got married in Bend. After our night in the snow, I thought of Drew more generously, but I still pitied whoever it was that married him. Meanwhile, I took a job flying aerial inspection over the oil pipelines. No more students and no passengers for me.

After Drew and his frozen toes—maybe since Liu, really—the notion to leave was knocking around in the back of my mind for some weeks. I worked a few more shifts on the fuel line, then I made what turned out to be my very last visit to the airport for a meeting with the FAA. At first it seemed the agents were keeping me waiting. I sat in the lounge, cataloging the passage of every minute for the better part of two hours before Manny shambled by and saw me and asked, exasperated, what was I doing there. As it turned out, the FAA had postponed our meeting. They'd sent word the afternoon before, Manny said. Once again, I hadn't been told. Normally it was Denise who'd relay those sorts of communications, but in this same communication that she might have relayed to me, the FAA had also delivered the recommended terms of Denise's firing. Denise was let go. Overburdened as she was with flight-school duties, airport duties, and her church work, too, a number of communications had slipped past her. The CAAC's recall of Liu Feng, for instance, had slipped past her.

After hearing all this from Manny, I took another look at the reception desk and saw it unmanned and the ceramic ducks that had once crowded it so impractically, gone also. I turned back to Manny with my fresh eyes and saw he had aged fifteen years overnight. His skin fit poorly, I thought, as if someone had squeezed all the meat and bone out of him, then stuffed him back into his skin. I sat there, looking from Manny's harrowed face to Denise's empty desk, and I saw there was nothing left for me. I think we hardly realize it, until afterward: how tenuously the idea of our life is trussed up, how flimsy the whole thing is, and how quickly, like clouds, it can dissipate and leave us a different person. I thanked Manny and left with an armful of shirts and papers that had been loitering in my locker for years, which I later threw away.

It isn't glamorous work that I left for, monitoring the pipelines, and it doesn't pay anywhere near as well as commercial might have, but there's skill involved. It takes a pilot who knows a few things. I'm looking for trouble on the pipelines, a rupture, people digging where they shouldn't dig. I'm flying low, one thousand feet off the ground, in mountainous country, low enough to spot a hand wave, hello, little plane, and fare-thee-well. From that distance, everyone is inclined to like you.

DIRTNAP

I WAS STAYING AT Jean's apartment in LA for a month to escape an especially dire Oregon winter and to test how much weight our relationship could bear. We'd been conducting a long-distance romance for nearly a year then—back-and-forth visits and little gifts in the mail, all the time texting, emailing every day, wagering all the money we had on the effort. If we performed all the steps in our elaborate ritual in exactly the right order, it was almost possible to conjure the other; to feel, rather than eight hundred miles apart, as though we were separated by a wall or a closed door. Jean happened to be better suited to this than I was. She possessed first-rate powers of object permanence. Her apartment looked like the inside of her beautiful head. She kept her front room crowded with plants. In the hall there was a hulking chifforobe with its doors missing, a beautiful old art deco piece from France by way of a thrift shop on Sunset Boulevard. At its bottom shelf, where the doors were missing, was a milk crate of old Polish folk records. She ate her meals at an extravagantly long dining table made by a woodworker she used to be in love with. When conversation dried up, we could talk about the trinkets on the shelf or the philodendrons gleaming in the window light, or we could patronize her little tabby cat, Cheever. Jeanie, in those day, wrote marketing copy for start-ups and published personal essays in magazines in her spare time. Mostly, they were hip online venues, but a couple old print titans you're surely familiar with.

Jeanie lived with an Australian woman named Indigo. I was never certain how Indigo survived in the world, especially in the high-rent landscape of LA. She ran sex and wellness workshops and associated with artist types. At the start of my California sojourn, Indigo invited us to her butt-plug party, which I was willing to attend as a sort of goof, but even Jeanie, as receptive to life as she was, had to blink at first. Indigo offered that it was basically a normal party, totally nonsexual, except that everyone would be wearing a butt plug like a happy little secret beneath their shorts. I told Indigo a butt plug was probably an improvement over the stick I usually wore up my ass at dinner parties. Graciously, she laughed, but I worried she didn't care for me too much. I'm a rat. I thought she could smell it, my reluctance of spirit and my disdain for joys I didn't understand.

Indigo drove a white panel van from, I guessed, the early nineties. She called it Dirtnap. The name was taken from some graffiti the van picked up while parked on a chain-link overpass above US 101. Someone was inspired to write *Dirtnap* on the passenger-side door. Before that, the van had been called Esmeralda, but one glance at the sinister-looking beater and there was no denying Dirtnap was the more suitable name. Every year or two Indigo took Dirtnap to the Home Depot parking lot to find a DIY contractor to remove the graffiti so that the police would stop pulling her over for every minor infraction. When pristine and white, Dirtnap might stay that way for months at a time, until someone spotted the empty canvas and christened it again with another first tag. Then the domino effect—one tag the first day, two more the second, three more the third, and soon the van took on the visage of a tagged-up boxcar. Indigo loaned Dirtnap to Jeanie and me on a few occasions. We drove to the hot springs out past Ojai and painted ourselves with black mud that smelled like eggs and lay naked in the shallow pools. We trekked out to Anza-Borrego for a wildflower super bloom in the slot canyons. Each trip saw a generous amount of sex in Dirtnap, for which Indigo expected no shame or contrition, nothing at all except that we refill the tank and wash the sheets of the bed in back.

Partway through this California sojourn of mine, Indigo was required back in Melbourne unexpectedly—her grandfather was on the way out after a fall in his garage. Indigo asked if Jeanie could move her van for street cleaning, and Jeanie promised we'd take care of Dirtnap as though it were our own.

Back then I worked as a content strategist for a failing mental health and substance abuse nonprofit. I worked remotely, and without any baked-in reasons to leave my home, I seldom did. I worried this was doing irreparable damage to me, which would make itself apparent only after the transformation was complete. It was an irony not lost on my friends that I should be writing self-care content, primarily for teens, when I maintained a lifestyle of such mis-care. I drafted business briefs, executive statements, interviews. I wrote PSA scripts for celebrity influencers no one had ever heard of. But mostly I wrote list-style clickbait. "10 Ways to Beat SAD" or "5 Ways You Can Help Prevent Bullying," "4 Ways to Make It through the Holidays after a Recent Loss," and so on. This was the other reason I went to LA. There was an upcoming mental health policy conference in Pasadena. I was going to attend with our video guy to capture some interviews and other content for our website.

The first day of the conference happened to be a Friday, which was street cleaning in Echo Park, though I didn't recall that at the time. Jeanie was opening the front door, on her way to the Arts District to meet a new client. Then she remembered Dirtnap.

"Shoot," she said. "Dirtnap."

"We have to move Dirtnap," I said.

"I'm almost late already. Could I ask you a favor?"

"Should I move Dirtnap?"

"Would you be comfortable doing that?"

She told me to remember to put on the steering club, because Dirtnap's ignition could be jimmied with any key. She left for work, and I took my chance to use her bathroom without feeling self-conscious about it, and then I went to see about parking. Already Dirtnap was the last vehicle on the left side of the street, and the right side of the street was very nearly filled with cars, except for one opening—a tight squeeze I doubted was at my skill level.

Dirtnap lacked side windows in the back, and the rear windows were covered with pink carpet. The walls and ceiling were stapled with carpet, too. She had the van turned into a little tin can of a bedroom. There were a few cubbies filled with several pairs of old sandals, and a low children's dresser, which was fastened into place with bungee cords. I had no experience driving anything larger than a compact pickup. The fact is, I wasn't a particularly strong parallel parker in the first place, which was not a truth I cared to admit to myself, but I did so now. I was raised in the open country of vast parking lots, their few cars and hundreds of seagull tenants looking lost and complacent. I pulled up alongside the last opening and cut in hard and blindly. Too hard, it seemed, after jackknifing into the curb. An

attempt beyond salvaging. I stepped out and paced around the perim-
eter of the van and said, "Okay, okay," then did the same thing again. I
tried a third time. Each attempt I told myself I'd try it a different way,
I would learn from my mistakes, but after trying again, it seemed I'd
done it the same wrong way. Now I was late, too, to meet my camera-
man. I felt like crying in frustration. I tried again.

A man came by and saw me having a tough time. I hoped the man
would keep moving and spare me an audience for my shame or else
just go ahead and carjack me and solve my trouble by making everything else worse. The man slowed his pace, then he stopped altogether
after watching me fail again. He put a hand on his hip and the other at
the back of his neck and stood there until I cranked down the window.
I saw then that he had only one ear.

"It's a tight one," I offered.

"It's a tight one, yeah, and that's a pretty big rig you're in."

"It's not mine," I said. "I'm not used to it. I'm not sure how far out
my ass is."

"I can see that."

"The windows," I said, thumbing over my shoulder. "She's got carpet on them. My view, it's super obstructed."

"Well, that don't help you any."

"What's someone need carpet on a window for?"

The man shrugged. "You come on back, and I'll tell you how much
space you got left."

My desperation took up so much mental space that there was nowhere left to entertain my dignity. It was a liberating feeling, almost.
The tension unlevered and I could breathe again, but I wasn't any
better a parker for it. I cut back in. The man said, "Keep coming,

now crank it, keep coming, crank it, all the way back, and yeah, keep cranking, more, more than that, you got, oh, oh, nope, hold on. Hold on. Want to pull back out and give it a fresh go?"

"It's tricky," I said. "I'm making a mess of it."

"Listen, if I wouldn't be stepping on your toes too much, I could just pull you in. I used to drive something like this for work."

"I don't want to take up your time," I said. I was already opening the door. "You can still save yourself."

He waved me off. "It'll take no time. Shoot, I'm not leaving a guy in a spot like this."

I put the parking brake on and stepped out and let the man climb in. I thanked him again and he said, "I'm going to straighten out and get a clean start." The man pulled out of my botched run and leaned out the window to look over his shoulder. "Okay," he said. Then he drove down the street and turned the corner. I stood silent at the curb for a few moments before wandering out into the street. I walked down to the corner and leaned out and looked around.

I'D BEEN UNDER the impression that the police never really located stolen beaters or even tried, but, as it happens, it only took them four days to find Dirtnap. Indigo had already arrived back from Melbourne by then, looking buoyant and bright-faced, because, although her grandfather had passed away and her van was stolen, she had made a new lover of a woman she'd met at a concert. Possibly, she said, there was something to this one. They were writing emails, making outlandish, intercontinental plans that no one would ever hold them to. I had never been so grateful for another person's good fortune. She stood in the living room in her orange pants, speaking with the police on the phone about her stolen van as blissfully as though they were congratulating her.

The van, the police said, was found parked at the curb three blocks from the apartment—so close I wondered if the thief hadn't felt remorse and tried to return it near enough that we might find it by accident. "The police were a bit snarky!" Indigo said. "They didn't come out and say it, but they all think I just forgot where I parked. I could tell." After locating the van, the police—this surprised me—didn't collect the vehicle themselves but told Indigo the location so that she could retrieve it on her own time. "What if meth heads are camped out in it?" we asked. Indigo had the same worry and told us that the police had told her, in so many words, *C'est la vie.*

So we went to find Dirtnap together on the street where the police said it would be, and there, at the curb, it was. We held our ears to the back door and heard nothing. Knocked and heard nothing. Indigo fished her spare keys out of her pocket. She paused and checked over her shoulder. It felt like stealing, she said in nearly a whisper. I imagined we'd find all sorts of things inside her van of horrors. Needles and spoons, condoms, soiled bedsheets, used toilet paper, jugs of urine, an overdosed man, a murdered woman. What we found were two trash bags overstuffed with women's clothing, a plastic grocery sack of toiletries stowed in the little dresser, and a pair of toothbrushes in a Ziplock bag.

"Well, shit, it was a woman!" Indigo said.

As she picked through the clothing, Jeanie said it was at least two women. She held up two bras of wildly different sizes. Indigo told Jeanie to be mindful of needles.

"I just never pictured a woman stealing a car," Indigo said. "Is that problematic?"

"Yeah, well, maybe it was still a man though," I said.

Jeanie turned to me with even more bras in her hands. "What makes you think so?" she asked.

I stood beside Dirtnap in a pickle of moral discomfort again. The thing is, I hadn't been completely truthful in my telling of events. The story, as I told it, saw Dirtnap stolen from its spot in my absence, after I had parked it dutifully and left for the conference. Afterward I came home and made a show of surprise and consternation for Jeanie that the van was not where it ought to be. I hurled myself into the apartment, asking, "Hey, Jean, did you move Dirtnap?" I didn't know I was capable of such a thing, and yet it came to me so naturally that I despaired for myself. My panic was heartfelt. Later Jeanie sat tense on the sofa as I paced about on the phone with Indigo, informing her about her van, that it seemed to be gone. Indigo needed to know when and where I'd parked for the police report, but I was having trouble producing anything except apologies.

"Avery, I'm hearing a lot of guilt in your voice," Indigo said. "And I want you to know this wasn't your fault."

I was unworthy of her kindness, and as a minor token of my guilt, I offered that I hadn't remembered to put the steering club back in place, and in that way, everything could be considered my fault. This had exactly the effect I'd intended—even more leniency, grace, pity. "Don't be so hard on yourself, Avery," she said—and this disappointed me terribly. What I wanted, it turned out, was for someone to really beat me up. I wanted someone who had saved up every mean thought she'd ever had about me to unload it all at once.

After we drove Dirtnap back to the apartment, Jean and I stood watching Indigo dig through the contents, trying to discern which was her trash and which the thief's. This wasn't the first time Dirtnap had been stolen, Indigo told us. Twice now, Dirtnap had gone missing, and twice the authorities managed to track it down. Indigo didn't seem at all astonished by the odds. She'd only been in the country four years. Maybe she thought this was a common feature of American life. You might think car thieves are looking to steal big-ticket items: Lamborghinis, or Teslas—I don't know cars very well—Hummers, maybe. Not so. Car thieves are on the lookout for Dirtnaps, it turns out—crusty old beaters already preparing to die of natural causes. The last time Dirtnap was stolen, the authorities rescued it from a chop shop in the nick of time.

What made it different this time, she said, what made it worse, was that the thief hadn't stolen Dirtnap to scrap for parts, but to make a home of it. Indigo spent the rest of the afternoon removing the thief's effects and, not knowing what else to do, put them out with the garbage. Indigo stripped the sheets and washed them twice, then she threw those away, too. By evening, Indigo seemed uncommonly sluggish. We sat on the sofa by the front window, which looked out over the curb, halfway expecting the thief, or thieves, to come by hunting for their lost belongings. "I'm not a prude," Indigo said, staring at a glass of wine in her hand. It wasn't the sex but the invasive part, she said, the violation of it. I ventured that perhaps it had been a platonic, no-sex scenario.

Indigo looked at me. "They kept their toothbrushes in the same baggie," she said.

*   *   *

THRILLVILLE, USA

THE FOLLOWING WEEK, Jean and I went to the natural history museum. We microdosed LSD, which made the world, though otherwise unchanged, seem to open its arms to me. We spent the afternoon standing in wonder before dioramas: a peep show of African elephants, a pair of Western bull moose, then the American bison, the Tibetan yak, the brilliant sage grouse looking alien in its fabulous plumage with its yellow chest inflated as taut as a balloon. In the foyer, dinosaur bones hung in the shapes of dinosaurs. The cafeteria was busy with foreign tourists, and we thought the coffee was pretty good. I hadn't known Jeanie had any interest in rocks, and then, in the gems and minerals hall, she pointed at the first podium, where three extravagantly beautiful gems sat in a glass case. She said, "Elbaite, beryl, and quartz, variety amethyst." I walked up to the information plaques and found she was correct. I couldn't believe it. First she only shrugged, then she lost herself to a giddy fit of laughter. Where'd she learn her geology? I don't know. I didn't think to ask. The LSD was still doing its work on me and I had no interest in untangling the mysteries of the universe. I led her through the whole exhibit, covering the plaques with my hands, making her guess. She named almost every rock in the room—spessartite, chalcedony, adamite, gold. Toward the end, a young boy grabbed the back of my jeans, and then, seeing I was not his father, fled wordlessly. Jean and I found everything hilarious and touching, especially this.

It was the finest afternoon I'd known in a long time, so generous in its loveliness that I felt mournful about it immediately. Standing over a millipede's terrarium—Jean crouched down opposite me, and I watched the fascination playing across her face through the glass—I said to myself, this is it, Avery. This is the afternoon against which you will measure all your afternoons to come.

We rode the subway home. We sat by the door, across the aisle from a woman with a young girl who kept a shivering dog between her feet. A few other people minding their business.

Jeanie leaned in as if she were about to share something sweet and private. "Someone thinks you're cute," she said. I turned to see, and she said, "Not now. He's still looking."

There was a man sitting kitty-corner to us, across the aisle, on the other side of the door, who looked away as I glanced over. You, I thought. It's you, the one-eared man, the Dirtnap thief. I should have felt, what—surprise? I didn't feel surprise. It was the strangest thing, as if someone had already told me this would happen and I'd forgotten and now had been reminded. Of course, I thought. It's you. But did he recognize me? The man sat like the statue of a man, everything about him stone-still but for his eyes, which twitched around the car, settling nowhere, as though he were tracking the movements of an invisible fly.

"Now he's feeling bashful," Jean said, laying her head on my shoulder. "Look away and I bet he looks again." I stared down at Jean's hands and mine in my lap, and then felt the man watching me again. I had to remind myself that the LSD wasn't entirely finished with me. "It's like future lovers at the bar," Jean whispered. "She catches his eye once and that doesn't mean anything. But a second time, well."

When I looked up again, the man had not yet turned away and we watched each other for a moment. Everything was electrified. The air even, it touched my skin with a buzz. Then the man made like he was sleepy. He hung his head over his folded arms, swaying a little as the car beat around a curve. We rushed on beneath the city. Tunnel lights flashed by the windows. My first thought was that maybe the universe was presenting me with a caution, or a reminder of how fortunate I was. All my life after this would be a gift of uncommon luck, or grace, and if I hazarded myself again to that same peril, I'd get what was coming to me.

I stared at the man as he pretended to sleep. "You don't recognize him," Jeanie asked, "do you?"

I did tell the whole story eventually. When I was made to.

The first of my troubles began with the keys. Indigo asked where had I put the keys after I parked Dirtnap. I hadn't considered that. Panic took me. Hadn't she used the keys, I asked, the other day, to pick up Dirtnap? But, no, she said. Those were the spare keys.

"Didn't I put the keys in the bowl?"

"That's what I'm trying to figure out," she said.

Indigo was suspicious, though she tried not to show it. She played coy as she built a case against me. It took her a couple of weeks to receive the surveillance footage from property management, by which time Dirtnap had already been located and she had no reason to look at the footage, except for a funny feeling. The apartment building had two surveillance cameras, one in the back, and one that happened to be pointed right at the stretch of curb where I'd said I parked Dirtnap. You see my trouble.

By the time it was all over, even the true story sounded half-made-up. Nobody thought me an outright villain, but what was the truth, what was a lie, and why had I gone to so much trouble to obscure the two, Indigo couldn't figure. Neither could Jeanie. She and I kept at it for a few months longer, but we never really recovered our old dynamic. I made one more visit to LA, a good-faith effort, but there was such a desperation about it. Jean often vanished into her thoughts, studying me as if I were a stranger in her living room, as if I might do anything next, pluck the magnets off the refrigerator and squirrel them into my mouth, upturn her potted plants to see what was buried inside. On one occasion, lying down to bed, Jean couldn't sleep and read instead in the chair beside the dresser, turning pages gently beneath a small lamp. Happening later to open my eyes, I found Jeanie staring at me above the open book in her lap, which she quickly took up and began to read again. With my eyes closed now, I listened to the sound of Jeanie turning a page every minute or so. Then, again, the pages stopped turning. She's watching me, I thought. In the middle of the night, wondering, who's in my bed? Or was she only sleeping there on her own in the armchair across the room, curled up as if protecting something, holding it close? I didn't open my eyes to see which.

But none of that had happened yet. I still believed I had survived everything. Everything was still ahead of me. Here it comes, the future, hold out your arms!

That afternoon in the subway car, the thief rose from his seat, and I thought he was coming to speak to me. I thought he was going to tell me a secret about my life. Dread welled up in me. Please, don't tell me, I thought. Keep all your secrets to yourself, because I don't want to know. Don't tell me how old I'll be when I die. Don't tell me how many more times Jean will appear in my doorway before never appearing there again. But then he turned and stood facing the door as the brakes kicked in beneath our seats. The car came to rest and the man stepped out and the doors closed behind him. He was sealed out into the world again, as good as gone. He turned and looked at me, one more time, through the window. He made no secret of it now, that he saw me, that I was exactly the man he thought I was. Then the window began to move and leave his hard, watchful face, and he disappeared into a sea of dim faces and moving forms. As we picked up speed, the tunnel swallowed us again and everyone was gone.

"No," I told Jean in the subway car. "That's not a man I recognize."

Then Jean laid her head back down on me, and from the tone of her voice, I knew she was speaking with her eyes closed. "You must just be pretty, then," she said.

SIX YEARS LATER I was living in Medford, Oregon. I was working as a content director for a hospital group. If ever I passed within a hundred miles of LA, I started to dream about Jean again, although she didn't live there anymore.

I saw on Facebook she had published a memoir in essays about her father's mental illness at a small press and was developing something of a name for herself. After the publication she landed a job as the writer in residence at a literary arts center in Seattle, where she taught community classes, gave occasional lectures, but mostly was free to do with her time as she pleased. It was the sort of job that comes with some prestige in the writing world but to the average citizen seems a sad station for a woman approaching forty.

I was required for an afternoon meeting in Seattle the same day Jean was scheduled to give a reading at her writer's house. The reading was hardly more than a half-hour walk from my hotel. My meeting ended early, and I had an empty evening ahead of me. Without giving it much consideration at all, I found myself on the sidewalk, heading north, and soon I'd arrived at the house's cramped little bookstore, where I hid myself behind the shelves like a pervert and tried my best to remain invisible. The owner of the store, when I arrived, was midway through Jeanie's introduction, listing her accomplishments and publications, which had grown more numerous and illustrious since we parted. I scanned the crowd for her, wondering if, for the sake of theatrics, they'd stowed her in the hall or a side room. Then I recognized the back of a head seated in the front row. Poor Jean always had trouble receiving compliments. I wished I could see what her face was doing as the shop owner praised her brilliance at length. When he'd finished with his spiel, he asked for applause, and Jean rose from her seat and turned to the crowd and thanked us all for coming. She had a slim book in her hand and, without much ado, she read to us. What can I say? How marvelous it was to see her again, and how strange it felt to witness her as a stranger, and how proud was I to have shared anything with her at all. My heart was pounding like crazy, my pulse thunking in my temple. I could hardly hold on to a word Jeanie read. I had this ransacking feeling as though I'd gone about life entirely the wrong way. I remembered an evening Jean and I spent years ago dissecting the patterns of our past romances. "You act like your life," Jean had said, "is just a story that happens to you. You're always looking for someone to tell you what comes next. Loving someone just because she loved you first." Somehow I mistook that for a compliment, I recalled now with a wince, as if she were praising my gladness to go with the flow. Then Jean left the room without saying anything else, leaving me confused and fearful with a sink full of dishes.

Then the reading seemed to be over. The crowd was clapping again. She'd worked her magic on the room. Everyone wanted a chance to tell her so. I bought a copy of Jeanie's book for her to sign. I hadn't bought her book at its publication, half a year prior, and I worried she'd smell the shame of it on me. I planned to tell Jean that my *other* copy of her book, the well-loved copy, dog-eared, coffee-stained, tearstained even, was at home in Medford, and that I hadn't expected to see her, hadn't expected a chance to have a book signed by her. In fact, I really hadn't considered the reality of seeing her at all, or what I'd say to her. And now, having come, I understood that I could not call it chance or accident. If I was here, I was here for a purpose. It occurred to me that I might make an escape still unnoticed. Then she spotted me and her face bloomed with that old, easy grace and I forgot myself entirely and went to her.

"I swear, Avery," she said. "I thought that was you. I saw you hiding and decided I'd just let you approach whenever you were ready."

I told Jeanie, "Look at you, Jeanie. Wow." Then we traded small, heartfelt pleasantries back and forth for a while, and when we'd run out of things to say, she offered to show me her apartment around the corner.

Jeanie's place was populated with all the old dressings I remembered from her apartment in LA—the hanging plants and windowsill succulents; translucent railroad insulator on the bookshelf; that big, beautiful table and the midcentury sofa, which was elegant and uncomfortable. I recognized a planter I had gifted her housing a new fern. The same art prints hung on foreign walls. It was as if her old apartment had been destroyed and someone had endeavored to piece it back together from the smithereens but could never get it quite right. Cheever, her cat, saw me and made a shrill peep, then stood to press his face against my leg until I picked him up. "Look at that," Jeanie said. I believed she was about to say that Cheever had missed me but thought better of offering up such a perilous thing. Jean's mother had passed away of Lou Gehrig's disease, I'd heard, not more than a year after our breakup. I thought I should say something about this but didn't know what, or how, and so instead I ate all of the olives she brought to me, popping them into my mouth one by one like a toad. And then, as if it were the most natural thing in the world, she came to me, removed the empty ramekin from my hand, and gently, with only her fingertips and not a word of explanation, pressed me to lie back on the sofa. For a moment I believed she might stoop to kiss me, but to my surprise she turned and lay down on her back on my chest, on the long hard sofa, and together we watched the light change on the ceiling as the sun went down redly. She rose and fell as I inhaled and exhaled beneath her. What a wonderful thing for one person to do to another, I thought.

"This part feels familiar," she said.

Later I followed her into the kitchen, where she went to make tea, and in the open doorway I was amazed at how easily it seemed we might slip back into old lives. I didn't understand why she was doing this with me. At this point, I think we both had the strong suspicion that at the least we were going to sleep together again, and this shared secret, in its unspeakability and lack of corroboration, held tremendous power over us. It had us sealed in a jar. Soon we were pushed into each other, pressed against the counter. Jean took the kettle off the burner and we went down on the laminate floor, yanking our clothes off. I wondered if we would move to the bedroom at some point, but it seemed we wouldn't, and I was relieved. I lay prone over Jeanie and felt the floor's crumbs and cat hairs grafting themselves to my forearms. I imagined her naked back must feel like the underside of the sofa cushion. Then, in the midst of this thing we were doing together, the cabinets seemed to be clattering, but why? At first I thought, it's us, we've set the room to shaking with our frantic lovemaking, but we were holding still now, I decided, and the room was still shaking. In the cupboard, stacks of dishes chattered like teeth. The floor buzzed urgently beneath us. Water agitated itself in a glass on the counter, and a cookbook slapped flat on the shelf above the sink. What is this? I thought. Are we dying? It was like being stoned out of the blue.

We were each searching the other's expression for an answer as to why the room was shaking. It wasn't computing, and then at the smack of another book, her face lit up, and mine, in recognition, and we understood. Oh yes, an earthquake. It was like sharing a dream. I saw my thoughts turning around in her eyes. And all was good, supremely good. All was in service to a grand pattern of goodness and rightness that lay far beyond our comprehension, and it was good and right to dissolve into it by the grace of God and forget oneself. The only thing I wanted to do was the only thing required of me. If a priest had entered the room right then, I would have asked him to baptize me on the spot in the bathroom's little shower. Then, all at once, the quaking passed and we entered into the stillness of old empty cathedrals, and in that pristine stillness Jeanie and I finished what we started.

Later Jean pulled her clothes on and set the cookbooks upright and fixed the cabinet doors shut. She even took the glass of water that had shaken and divvied it out into her hanging plants. I ached with the mystery of where she had gone to now in her head, into which I had glimpsed once and feared I would not glimpse again. I asked her what she was thinking so numerously in the next hour that she finally put a hand over my mouth. An earthquake, in the middle of earnest nooky business, and how am I expected to believe all of this, the whole world, everyone in it, isn't a story about my life?

The bigheaded feeling would not release me. It had eaten me alive. I thought it had hold of Jeanie, too. We discussed my flight gingerly, which was scheduled for first thing in the morning. I said it wouldn't be terribly hard to push it back a day. She asked, "What's the rush?" So I canceled my ticket and purchased another to the morning after next.

WE SPENT THE next day and a half telling each other the story of the earthquake over again and again, until we'd settled into the most agreeable way of telling it, so that it was readily reproducible, so that it emphasized just exactly what we wanted it to—the clap of the book, the way we looked at each other all through it, the realization, the exquisite stillness that followed, and how, with patience and generosity, we managed to climax at the same time. And then the narrative began to balloon in its significance, its grandiosity, the depth of its implications, until it started to ring hollow, after which point we had nothing left to talk about with much honesty, and conversation deserted us again. We went out for dinner and spoke mostly about the food. We sat at a table by a window overlooking the Puget Sound. An oversize Ferris wheel stood at the end of the pier, turning its lights high on the evening dimness. Our drinks were finished. The sun was low on the sound and cast a pebbled trail of sunset out on the water, seeming to end there at our feet, as if we might step out and follow it somewhere bright and painless.

"My mom passed away," Jean said, "a few years back. I don't know if you heard that or not."

"Ah, Jeanie, I wanted to say something. Shoot," I said. "This whole time, I wanted to say something, but I didn't know what."

"I could tell you did," she said. "I thought you were about to say something earlier."

"I was being a coward about it," I said.

"You don't have to say anything else about it," Jeanie said. "It just feels funny not to mention it."

"I'm sorry, Jeanie. When I heard, I really did want to call you, but."

"I know," she said. "Thank you."

We were silent again. A waiter came and asked if we would order anything more and Jean said she thought we were about to head out. Then Jean told me her mom had continued to mention me into her final days.

"Oh no," I said.

"Don't worry," she said. "It wasn't anything bad. Mom wasn't keeping up," she said, "up here," and touched her fingertips to her own temple as tenderly as if it were her mother's. "Some days she thought I was still in LA. She thought we were still running around together. Other times she did remember more, I think, and those times she still thought everything was okay. She said, 'People fight, Jeanie. People make up, Jeanie. People keep coming back around to each other like they've done.'" Jeanie went to drink from her glass, but it was empty. "She really hoped I'd be married before she passed. The least I could do was let her think we might come back around to each other. Was that dishonest? Should I feel icky about that?"

"Well, but, here we are," I offered.

"I guess so," she said. "I also told her I'd made my way back to religion."

"Have you?"

"Oh no," she said, and laughed. "But I think I may have believed it when I said it."

* * *

THE NEXT MORNING, at the onset of rush hour, Jeanie drove me to the airport. We spent a half hour stalled by traffic. The world looked beautiful and filled me with sorrow. The low sun split itself over the mountaintops and fell in a fan of white light down through morning haze. But there was only so much conversation we could pull from the fineness of the morning, and then again we fell beneath that tyranny of silence. What a shame that it must be so hard to say one thing you mean to a person with whom you have shared all your secrets already. I had that racing feeling in my chest again. It wasn't too late to call it all off. We could turn back at any exit. Someone must only say it, I thought. Then Jeanie began to scream.

There was a dog in the road. A pit bull with a great block of a head. The poor dog had been struck by a car, but it wasn't dead yet. The dog lay bloodied and limb-mangled in the middle lane, craning its head wildly in pain and terror. I had never heard an honest scream from Jeanie, a true exaltation of horror, and was shaken by it now. Already the dog was behind us. Jeanie slowed down, but the flow of traffic at our rear kept us moving down the highway. She changed to the right lane as if she might pull over, but she didn't. She asked if I'd seen it, the dog.

"What do we do?" There were tears in her eyes, which she kept pointed at the road ahead.

"I don't know if there's anything we can do."

She asked if we should pull over, and again I said I didn't know what we could do for the poor dog. I thought the dog was dead by now. Behind us the traffic was thick and moving quickly. If the dog hadn't died from the initial collision, then the cars that followed had already finished the task. As a boy, I was taught that dogs prefer to die alone.

"We could wave down traffic."

"That's one possibility," I said, "but I don't know where we'd wave them to."

She said we could call the police to . . . well, she didn't know what, but we could call. There was a car I'd seen, already pulled over, I said, who I guessed was the unfortunate driver that hit the even less fortunate dog. He had probably called already, I suggested. At this point, we knew, the urgent danger wasn't the dog's, but the oncoming commuters who might swerve in avoidance and wreck against the high cement median. The longer we speculated, the farther away we were from it all, and the more irretrievably dead the dog. I watched Jeanie, wondering what she might do next, but she seemed to be waiting on me. Then I understood that Jeanie couldn't be the one to decide to pull over. To do so would guarantee I miss my flight. If we were to pull over, it would have to be my decision and my sacrifice.

I also understood, right then, as plainly as anything in my life, that if I allowed her to drive me to the airport without a word of protest—if we did anything at all except go back to stand at the side of the road together and watch the poor dog die in agony and fear— then I would never see Jeanie again. An earthquake, a slain dog, a tepid goodbye in the drop-off lane, and that would be the very end of us. I wondered, would she step out of the car to kiss me farewell? Had everything been my fault, my decision? Well, time may make a fool of me yet, but it seems like I had it right. That was the last I saw of Jeanie.

COOPER GOES TO THE COUNTRY

OOPER WAS GOING to rehab again. Mom made the arrangements. All Cooper had to do was show up and suffer; all I had to do was make sure he got there. I drove even though it was Cooper's two-hundred-dollar Pinto. I only had the movies to go on and I'd never seen a man drive himself to rehab in the movies. I was also just a little worried that if Cooper were behind the wheel, he might change his mind at the last minute and drive me all the way to Acapulco.

Cooper had sensed that something like this was going on in my head. He's little brother. I'm big sister. That grants us both very minor powers of mind reading. He was a terror growing up, but in recent years—as he'd gone on devising novel and more inventive ways to burn his life to the ground, and as I'd more or less become recognizable as an adult—he'd begun to do as I said. At the driver's-side door, Cooper had held his hand out for the key, but I shrugged and did something funny with my lower lip instead. "I'll drive," I said. "You can stare out the window and feel as bad as you'd like."

He smiled coldly. He had a great talent for smiling coldly. Maybe he'd thought of something vicious to say, but he laughed instead. This is where, if it were Mom driving him a second time, he'd chew her head off for sport. Not all his fault. Mom is the way she is, and this was, for a second time, the lowest point of my brother's life. But it was me with him now. There's no sport in eviscerating a well-meaning sister; she doesn't care how you reflect on her; she has her own troubles and she's made room for yours. Cooper ignored me most of our lives, but he never had fun being mean to me. I cried too easily. I took things to heart. "Worried I'll get cold feet?" he asked.

"No, not so much," I said. "I just figured you look like shit, so I'd let you mope if you wanted." Cooper really did look awful. His color was bad. His hair was limp on his forehead and going thin at his crown. Get Cooper around a mirror and it ruined his mood for the day.

I hadn't seen Cooper for nearly three years then. We lost track of him for months at a time. The last I'd heard from him was only through Mom as intermediary. I call her every Sunday, and one such Sunday, Cooper had come around asking for money. She said, "Guess who I got here? I got your brother. Say hi to Lorrie. Did you hear that, Lorrie? Cooper says, 'What's up?'"

A little shy of a year after that, Cooper gave me a call and then he showed up at my door heaped in misery and we were brother and sister again. I'd agreed to give Cooper my spare room for three weeks under the condition that he get his shit together. Mom loved that. Cooper hated that Mom loved it, but he needed the room. If after three weeks his shit was just a little more together, I said, we could renegotiate the length and terms of his stay (an extended curfew, outings surpassing three hours would no longer require a phone call check-in, possibly an add-on to my cable subscription); otherwise, I was with Mom and Dad: Cooper would go to rehab again. Then three weeks go by and I'm here driving Cooper to rehab again. We're all adults. Cooper made a lot of noise, but in the morning he was there with his bags packed at the door.

We drove the first leg more or less in silence, with the stereo broken and a persistent funk in the air. You vomit in a car just a couple times and it never really bounces back. We could talk all day about that car and the things it'd been party to. The conversation ends, naturally, with Cooper's old buddy Denny, the hulking dope—this big blond boy with a head the shape of an upturned bucket—who overdosed in the back seat, years earlier, dead at twenty-five. He was sweet enough. I'm sorry Denny's dead, relieved he's gone. I just wish Cooper had never met him. They'd both have been better off without the other there to egg them on. I had wondered if the car would feel haunted, but it just felt like my brother's car, no more or less haunted than my brother. I would have taken my little Toyota, very clean, highly functional, but it was Cooper's trip and he wanted it to be his gas we spent on it. Maybe he held out hope the Pinto would break down halfway and we'd just throw in the towel and take a bus home.

I was feeling bad because I had hoped I'd come up with something compassionate to say. This seemed to be one of those definitive moments in a relationship, one in which assurances of love or admissions of admiration were due or at least counted for double. Nothing was coming to mind. I don't know. You'd like to think you could give the people you love just a little courage if you really wanted to. I was relieved to see that Cooper appeared to be in a poor mood for it anyway. He laid his head on the window as sad as a child and battled silently with his inexpressible despairs of missing things that were bad for him. We took the highway out of Salem, out through the low I-5 corridor and up the Santiam Pass into the mountains. The clinic was really out there some ways into the country, it seemed, to dissuade any patients from stepping out for a cigarette and ending up on a bus.

After the landscape had changed a few times over, which impressed upon us the distance we were going, Cooper stated the obvious. "Remote, this place." Yes, I thought, you could not trudge off to a friend's house from this one, if that's what he meant. Cooper would have to stay put.

"Like a resort," I said.

"I feel like an old dog getting his last ride out to the country."

"I can't tell if you're talking about euthanasia or what."

"Yeah, that's what I was getting at."

"I think you should think of it more like a resort. The reviews say the food's terrific compared to other places."

"Lorrie, you could sit me down at Ruth's Chris and feed me a groundhog right now," Cooper said, "and I wouldn't even know you're messing with me."

When Cooper saw I thought that was funny, he laughed too. I'd always thought Cooper was funny. If Cooper hadn't been funny, he would have gotten himself beaten to death by nineteen. I told him the clinic cost as much as a resort. Mom had to tell somebody.

"Well, it's her money," Cooper said. "However she wants to spend it. That's her deal. Not for me, though. You'd think she found me in the gutter. Just give me a bath."

"I don't know, Coop. That sounds like big talk for a guy who almost burned to death and froze to death in a single night. Usually, it's one or the other," I said. "That is a feat of a screwup, Cooper."

Cooper barked one good laugh and seemed to surprise himself. "I hadn't thought of it like that. Shit," he said. "I think you're being a bit dramatic about it, but, yeah, I hadn't thought of it like that."

Was I, though, being dramatic? I'd found Cooper deranged in my spare room a few nights before, at least drunk enough that he wasn't able to read my prescription label, or else he'd have known my pain pills weren't good for anything except managing UTI symptoms. Is your kitty burning, little brother? The bottle was open on the floor and the garbage can was on fire. Either he'd tossed a cigarette in it or he'd gotten cold and couldn't find the thermostat. By the time I doused my spare room with the fire extinguisher, Cooper wasn't around to see the mess. He left all his earthly possessions where they lay and left the door wide open to the cold. A bit of snow on the ground and the roadside ditch-water just about covered with a paper film of ice. It was winter. Cooper absconded in just his shorts. I saw a pale back wandering at the shoulder a half mile off, as reflective and bright in the moonlight as a road sign.

"No, listen," I said. "If it was your brother trying to kill himself on your watch, okay, and you remembered it, then you come talk to me about what's dramatic."

He raised his hands. "I know," he said, light and dismissive at first, but then again, more seriously, "I know. I know."

"Dramatic," I said.

He smiled. He had a cracked tooth at the bottom of his smile, which he'd been trying to hide. I wondered when that had happened, but decided I'd wait to press him on it. There was never a good time to bring anything up with Cooper. We went a while in silence again, as was our way. Three weeks together and we hardly got further than the weather. Oh, but it's sad, isn't it, to be returned to your family after your long years apart—to have dragged yourselves back to one another through your own versions of hell, and your brief heavens, the long valleys between, accumulating on your way all these stories you'd so love to confide in the first people of your life, and tell them what you've seen—only to find you have returned as strangers in your hearts? I wished so much for my little brother, and none of it had reached him. Nothing good had ever happened for him. Whose fault, it didn't really matter.

THE MOUNTAIN PASS took us through a many-years-now burned-down pine forest, which looked especially ghostly in the snow, bone-yard, pristine, and an empty sky for miles and miles. Cooper watched everything with boredom and horror. The road was ours except for a motorcyclist who was making me nervous. I said it was too slick out here to hang on my bumper like he was—a figure of speech and doubly so, for there was no bumper to hang on to. The bumper had never wanted to stay put. I'd already told Cooper that was a guaranteed way to get pulled over. Cooper said he'd figured that out. "How do you think I got my one and only DUI? Not because of my driving." He could parallel park on mescaline if he wanted to.

"He's really hot on my tail, this jerk," I said. The motorcyclist was riding up on me, then backing off, riding up again, in a little tantrum, his face all pinched up, I'm sure, with hatred behind his helmet.

"He wants to get around you."

"Okay, so get around me, then," I said.

"He wants you to let him get around you." And it was true: I was in the middle of the road. There was some snow at the shoulder that I didn't want to mess with on Cooper's bald tires.

"Think I should brake check him?"

"Lor, my nerves are all fried out, man. This guy's going to make me puke in my lap."

I slowed down and hugged the shoulder just so this asshole could get on with his day and fail to learn any lessons from it, but then the motorcyclist continued right on into the back of the Pinto anyway. I felt a little jump in my seat and I heard the motorcyclist's helmet kiss the back window with a light clack. Then he dropped from view.

He seemed okay, thank God. Cooper and I watched at the side of the road, turned around in our seats. By the time we'd come full stop, the motorcyclist was already lifting himself from the ground and getting steady on his feet. He couldn't seem to get his helmet off.

"I was letting him go around," I said.

"I don't think he noticed."

"I was just getting over for him." I found it perfectly impossible to understand the very obvious thing that had just happened.

"If it seems like I'm imagining anything," Cooper said, mostly to himself, "somebody better clue me in." He looked at his reflection in the mirror. "Okay, well, let me go check on this fucker." Then he stepped out into the cold, closed the door behind him, and approached the motorcyclist. Cooper called to the man, "You in one piece, buddy?" The motorcyclist, when he caught sight of Cooper, started stomping over to him like a man on his way to murder a dog. Cooper saw all this too late. The motorcyclist was coming at him, and Cooper said, "Buddy?" and then my brother was punched in the face by an incensed motorcyclist in the snow in the middle of nowhere. The motorcyclist might have given him another, but Cooper bent over with his head in his hands and hacked a thread of bile into the road, then stood gripping his knees and retched for a few. I was out of the car by now.

"That's my brother," I said, as if it might clear up some misunderstanding.

"Ow, man, ow," Cooper said. "I wasn't even driving."

The motorcyclist, with a reflective visor over his face, turned from Cooper and pointed his whole head at me so that I seemed to be in the dim fishbowl of his thoughts, but he did not have the posture of a man who was about to attack a woman. He threw his hands up. I think he only had the good one punch in him anyway. He turned back to his motorcycle where it lay on the road and tried to pull it back right side up, but the front wheel, I'm sure he saw, was visibly the wrong shape. To make matters more difficult, he was a fairly small one. His helmet made his head look large for his body, like a furious toddler in leather. He hardly got the thing upright before he fell back off it and kicked the bike's undercarriage with his boot heel. We watched for a while, silently, as this stranger performed his ceremony of impotent rage, heaving his motorcycle about the asphalt, until finally he stripped his gloves off and got his helmet unbuckled and tossed that down at the beaten motorcycle. Then he turned to us. His hair stood in a thin poof above his head. He was so angry he had tears in his eyes. Cooper took a handful of dirty snow and held it at his temple.

"Are you cooling off yet?" Cooper asked. "Because I want to, like, discuss the situation with you, except I don't want to get punched in the head again."

"Yeah, I'll punch you right in the head again, man," the motorcyclist said.

"I wasn't even driving!"

"You drove into us," I added, feeling more comfortable now that I saw how much larger Cooper was than the man, though unwell and as slender as a spear of asparagus.

"They call that *at fault*," Cooper said, "whoever you ask." Then he turned and inspected his car at the place of impact, cool and insolent as was his style. I thought the little motorcyclist was going to take his head off and throw it at us. I'll be clear: the way the Pinto looked, this was a car you could have just pulled out of a lake yesterday. You could pop a tire and, the way the valuation worked out, they might just call it totaled. "Shoot, you even knocked my bumper off," Cooper said. "I don't even see where it went to."

I returned to the heated car and polished my hatred for the man, this petulant child in a little man's body, now that I'd decided none of it was my fault. Meanwhile, Cooper helped him drag the bike to the little snowbank at the side of the highway. The motorcycle made a very expensive-sounding scraping noise over the asphalt. No helping that. After a few more minutes, speaking at the side of the road, the pair of them came up to my window. I rolled it down.

"You're not going to like this," Cooper said. "So the thing is, there's no service up here."

As bad news goes, that didn't make itself apparent to me. Cooper registered as much by my face. "Bill can't get a line on a tow. That's his name," Cooper said, holding a thumb back at the motorcyclist. "This asshole is named Bill."

WE WERE THREE now. The mountains emptied out into the high desert and snow wasn't an issue anymore. At about fifty miles an hour, the Pinto would start to groan in protest. It made a sort of metal-wrenching sound as though it might disintegrate at any moment and leave you skidding down the highway in just the driver's seat, with the steering wheel still in hand like in the cartoons. It bothered our passenger. He sat sulking in the back seat, cradling his punching arm gingerly. "This is a real heap of shit," he said after giving it some thought.

"Isn't she?" Cooper said over his shoulder.

"Smells bad in here."

"Yeah, it's the only good two hundred dollars I ever spent."

"We can let you out," I said. "I'd prefer to have you walk."

"I'm just saying," the man said. "It smells like something died in here."

I glanced over at Cooper, but he was futzing with the mirror to see if he was bruising yet. "I was hoping to show up in good shape," he said. He pushed his hair up to see an ugly yellow coloring his skin. "I walk in there with a messed-up face and people will think I got serious problems. I even thought about it this morning: at least I'm not going in with a messed-up face this time."

I said I guessed they'd have figured out his problems bruises or not. Cooper was not so good at hiding himself as he thought he was. Then the motorcyclist hissed over his arm in the back seat. I asked if he landed on it in the crash.

"I guess I did," he said. "I didn't feel it at first."

"Well, your adrenaline's worn off," I said. "After your macho-macho bullshit."

"Actually, you know, I think I might have cracked it on your head," he said, speaking to the back of Cooper's head.

"I was just wondering if that was it," Cooper said.

"It's getting all puffy on me," the man said, raising his bad arm with his other for us to see the swelling. His knuckles were purpling.

"I'll count it as the first fight I ever won," Cooper said.

I'd have liked to press assault charges on Bill, but Cooper would have found that quaint. Instead of the tow shop, now we were going to leave Bill at the hospital. Bend was the nearest town with a hospital, but the turnoff for the rehab clinic was some thirty miles ahead of it. It used to be a ranch, the clinic. It had a very ranch aesthetic in the brochure. Pet and feed the horses, connect with the country, and so on, chickens and bullhorns mounted high and plenty. Mom's a great sucker for the country shtick—she's an indoor cat who's always thought of herself as an outdoor cat without justification. It left us a decision to make as to our passenger, though, this Bill person. I was prepared to drop Cooper off and drive Bill a ways farther on my own. I had this fear that if we passed the clinic we'd never make it back. Cooper said no to that. He turned back to Bill. "You get me, Bill. You've already shown yourself to be a violent man."

"I just got hot," Bill said.

"Just for my peace of mind, we'll drop me off on the way back," Cooper said. "Or else I'll have a cow."

I said I wasn't so worried about Bill.

"Yeah, well, I bet Bill's got a knife on him. Hey, Bill, you got a knife on you?"

Bill patted his pocket. "I always got my knife on me."

"It'll just be another half hour," Cooper said. "And, you know, you could walk me in there for a bit if you wanted. Not everyone does, but a lot of the people in there, someone walks in with them. They do the whole look-around and goodbye deal, the family stuff."

"Are you sick?" Bill asked. "Hell, I thought maybe you were sick. I thought, this is one of those young guys that's got cancer, and then I hit you anyway."

"No, Bill, I am going to rehab. I've got to dry out if I'm ever going to get my tolerance back down to earth."

"Oh, rehab," Bill said gravely, and with an air of knowingness, I thought.

"Yeah, well, you still picked a real fine day to punch me in the head."

"I thought maybe you were just sick."

"I'm only sick in the religious way, Bill. Except I guess I have been seeing stuff lately I haven't seen before. New, like, bodily developments. Not so encouraging stuff. So who knows, but I'm trying not to worry my sister here."

"Yeah?" I said. "That's for me? Coop, tell me this: Were you peeing red the other day?"

He looked shocked, as if I just spoke aloud something he'd heard said in his dreams. "What?" he said, aghast.

"Your pee," I said, "was it bright red?"

"I don't—"

"Because those pills you stole from my cabinet—"

"No, no, I thought about it. I had the bottle, yeah, but I didn't take any. I swear on my life. You can count them."

"Well, because those UTI pills," I said, "they make your pee go bright red." Which was true. My doctor had even warned me, and it still freaked me out. Cooper thought very hard about this with a stupid look on his face and then he started laughing. He held his chest to stop from exploding in his seat.

"Oh my God," he said. "I thought I was a goner. I thought I was peeing all my blood out."

"They won't get you high, but they'll make your pee red."

"I don't know," he said, still laughing, "I think I felt a little something."

"I promise you didn't."

"I thought I'd finally done it to myself. My God, I don't even know what I'm going to rehab for now. I'm cured. You hear that, Bill? I'm going to live forever."

We passed the turnoff for the rehab clinic a little farther on. Cooper saw the exit go by, and he turned to me with a little smile on his face. It was a smile I remembered on him from the holiday dinner table, when the prayer was being said, and sneaking open an eye, as I couldn't help but do, there's Cooper watching me with that smile, waiting for me to see and, in that very minor but lasting way, to enlist me in his cahoots.

IT'S A VERY flat landscape after the mountains, and Bend appeared all at once, more developed since we'd been here last as kids; a ski town in the winter, and in the summer, I didn't know what. I was ready to say goodbye to everyone and finish a bottle of wine by myself without ending the world. I took the freeway out to the east end of town where St. Charles was, and Cooper told Bill over his shoulder that before we got to the drop-off lane, they'd probably want to exchange insurance information. Dubious though, it seemed to me, that Cooper was up on his insurance payments. Cooper likes to mess with people. Bill grinned in the rearview mirror. He said he thought maybe Cooper had forgotten.

"All right," Bill said, "fine, all right. It's in my wallet here. I just gotta— You know, you never wake up thinking, hey, maybe I'll break my hand today, but then you wake up and—bam!—you run into some beater and your hand's broken and you have to pay for the privilege."

Bill had some trouble, it looked, getting around his bad arm to his jacket pocket. We were at an intersection on the freeway then, stopped for a light, and Bill was hunting around in his agony for his wallet when he popped the door open instead and ran off into traffic. Horns went mad before I understood what had happened. We sat there for a minute watching the man dodging cars artlessly, cradling his arm as he shambled off into a commercial plaza like a baby snatcher.

"My God," Cooper said, reasoning it out a moment after me. Next thing, Cooper had his seat belt off and a foot on the road. "No, you don't!" he said. "No, no."

I called after my brother, but he was after Bill now. He was off on foot shouting Bill's name. The light was green, and I'd accumulated some traffic behind me. Bill disappeared behind a sandwich shop, and Cooper after him. I called out to Cooper, "Just let him go," but both men were gone by then. The horns continued for me now. I had to step out of the car and scramble around its front to close the passenger door. I had my pick of reasons to curse my brother, but, in the moment, with the horns and the scolding strangers, what I hated him for most was leaving the door open. He couldn't be bothered to close the door.

Cooper left his phone in the car on the seat. He might as well have jumped out of an airplane. By the time I turned around and doubled back to the plaza lot, the two of them were long gone. There I did cry. Not in a concerted way, only tearful cursing, smacking the driving wheel. I looked like a lunatic to a young mother with her little child passing by my window. She averted her eyes. Not the little child though. He looked at me with genuine concern. I was older than his mother, which seemed like a fluke. When had that become the case?

I was older than all the young mothers. Were I on my own mother's timeline, I'd have had two by now.

I drove a couple laps around the place, then I went by the hospital just to be sure but saw no sign of them. I was inclined to get conspiracy-minded about my misfortune—who was that Bill guy, really, and where had Cooper found him and how much was he paid? By now the sun was setting a pink and dazzling way, and there was a phone call I dreaded to make, to Mom, to tell her I'd lost her boy. And how long, I wondered, would I stay before driving back home with Cooper's car and no Cooper? I drove back to the stretch of freeway where my luck had run out and parked in the nearest lot, which is where I found him, my only and lonesomest brother. I spotted his head back on a bench, facing the Lava Lanes bowling alley. People came and left as he sat there. I said aloud in the car, thank God, thank God. It wasn't just that I didn't want Cooper to die, but especially I didn't want him to die on my watch. Some things there are no helping, but, please, I beg you, as a sister, don't let it be my fault. I parked the Pinto and approached him from behind and wanted to kiss him.

"I was sure you were gone," I said. "I was driving back and forth and back and forth." I pointed at the road, but Cooper kept his eyes on the bowling alley.

"Yeah, I saw that," he said.

I stood beside him at the bench for a while and when he didn't say anything I sat down. I asked him if Bill got away from him, and he nodded. "What would you have even done if you caught him?" I asked.

"I have no idea. Kill him maybe," Cooper said. "I was mostly joking anyway. Thought he might give me twenty bucks if we agreed to forget it, but . . ." Cooper shrugged. He looked ahead at his reflection in the bowling alley window, through which a lighted Budweiser sign shone harshly in blue and white.

"Were you debating it?" I asked.

"I thought maybe I'd get one more game in," he said. I kept looking at him, and Cooper rolled his head over to me. The skin at his temple was taking on a deep color where Bill had punched him. "You can smell my breath if you want," he said.

"I just think, I don't know, a promising sign, yeah? You could have thrown this whole thing off the rails if you wanted to," I said. "It's good behavior."

"Lorrie, I swear I've gone on too long patting myself on the back for the bare minimum."

"I don't know. It gives me a good feeling."

"You know what the relapse rate after treatment is," Cooper asked, "even at a posh spot like this? It's like ninety percent, wherever you go. Ninety, man. Since when have I ever made it into the top tenth percentile?" He laughed sourly.

I told Cooper I didn't know who was giving him his facts, and he said he'd looked up studies after his first failed experiment with sobriety. "Back when I was trying to figure out what the hell happened, you know, and what was it that made me such an irredeemable piece of shit. But it turns out the whole business model for these places is more like a revolving door kind of logic. They've found a pig you can eat two or three times."

Cooper sat dead eyed, with nothing in him to cry about. My courage failed me here to confront the thing he was confronting. No, I said, I didn't believe that. "You feel that way now," I said, "because you're miserable. When you get out, though—if you just imagine that far ahead—it won't seem as true then. Two months sober and it will feel like a new world."

Cooper sat up straight and turned to me with urgency for once and he said, "Exactly. That's the messed-up part, Lorrie. When I walk out of there, numbers will just be numbers again. I'll believe in God and karma. I'll really think that this has made all the difference, but it won't. That's what I'm saying."

I told Cooper that's what anyone on his way to rehab says, but of course, Cooper was more or less right about all of it. I knew it when he said so, that in two months he would step into the clinic lobby to meet me, as right as rain, with his bag over his shoulder, a bit filled out since last I saw him, sheepish and stooped beneath that weight one bears when they emerge into a room in which they've just been spoken about. What he'd said to me outside the bowling alley was no less true or false, but we agreed, by way of never mentioning it again, that it hadn't mattered as much as we thought. There was no use in trying to fix the future before it arrived because, look around: there was so much to feel good about. It was a perfectly blue-in-every-direction day in the high desert. Cooper's skin was brighter than I'd seen it in years and he hugged me like he meant it.

When I drove Cooper to my apartment from rehab, back to Salem—I'd taken my car this time—we spent the trip discussing his future. Four weeks into his stay at rehab, he said he started making plans. He wanted to garden, first of all. He said all the cleaned-up drunks kept gardens. Maybe he'd get an old greyhound once he had a place for it, one of the sad old racing dogs to practice his kindness on. He wanted to find a job, and a girlfriend too, maybe a single mother, he said, someone who had already learned to want the small good things he was now committed to wanting. Then Cooper asked me to guess who called him at rehab, but I couldn't begin to guess. I didn't think Cooper had any friends left in the world.

"Glenn did," Cooper said. "Me and Denny's boss, from the old days. I guess Mom ran into him, told him where I was."

"Yeah? And what did Glenn want?" I was worried he'd made Cooper a job offer on another dim-witted business venture. Before Cooper's wayward, wandering years, he worked for Glenn at the roadside amusement park. By then Glenn had already managed to run a number of businesses into the ground. He had a soft spot for Cooper and he let Cooper take advantage of it. He even let Cooper stay on his couch for a spell. But then Denny died and Cooper took off and Glenn gave up on the park, and now, in its place, there's a mobile home community called Hope Valley.

"Glenn just wanted to see how they were treating me. He was a little drunk, I think, and there was a dream he'd had that he wanted to tell me about. That's what he really called for. In the dream, he said, he and I are on some sort of boat in the Arctic, and Denny's there, too, and we're all playing cards at night, but each hand we turn over is a three-way tie. He said we keep turning over the exact same hand, and each time it gets funnier and funnier—we bet everything and we get it back each time—and by the end it's like it's a spiritual feeling. We believe in God and we understand that the boat is taking us to heaven. We're already dead, but it's no worry."

"And then did he tell you what it all meant, or?"

"No, no," Cooper said. "He wanted *me* to tell him what it means. I said, I don't know, Glenn. Maybe I had to be there." Cooper laughed.

"He told me that he was unemployed, and even if he had a job to give, he wouldn't give it to me, but I've stayed there in his head, he said, all this time, as one of the voices he talks to when no one's around. He said he wanted me to know that while I was out there in rehab or worse, there are people still carrying me to heaven in their heads."

ACKNOWLEDGMENTS

A lot of support went into this book, such as it is, and I'm immensely grateful to everyone who lent me their help and encouragement. I owe a debt of gratitude to these that follow:

Henry Dunow, my agent, without whom this book would not have seen the light of day. My editor, Sean Manning, whose wonderfully refined sensibilities have brought out the very best in my work. I also owe much to the Writing Seminars at Johns Hopkins University, the creative writing program at the University of Wisconsin–Madison, Oregon Literary Arts, the Bread Loaf Writers' Conference, and all the terrific people therein who offered me support just when I needed it. And my teachers who encouraged me: Eric Puchner, Jean McGarry, Alice McDermott, James Arthur, and Matt Farrell.

And to my writerly friends that have persisted with me—J.P. Grasser, Cody Ernst, Maddy Raskulinecz, Matt Morton—I say, thank goodness for you. What a gift you've been to me. At the beginning, as throughout, I had the bottomless support and love of my family: Doug and Lisa, my parents; Andrew and Brent, my brothers and my first and closest friends; and Wanda, my grandmother, whom we call Oma.

ACKNOWLEDGMENTS

A good part of these stories I've stolen from their poorly guarded anecdotes.

And to Joselyn Takacs, my wife, first reader, brilliant editor, astonishing talent, and my dearest friend: this book, and my life, would have been so much less without you.